# HER CAROLINA PASSION

A Passion novella

---

GRACIE GUY

Her Carolina Passion © 2019 Gracie Guy

## About the Story

*When widowed Lizbeth Spensor agrees to a summer teaching English as a New Language (ENL) in South Carolina, her only plan is to come home with a killer tan. But a chance encounter at a* **Piggly Wiggly** *– seriously, who names these stores? – with Beau Landry stirs up action in her body parts she thought were long dead. But can a Northern gal who'd been with just one man in thirty years allow herself to melt under the honeyed voice of this salt and peppered titan of Southern industry?*

*To my SC family at the Pineapple Palace – thank you for one of the best vacations I've had in a very long time. I'm looking forward to Beach 2020!*

*To GMR Sr. – part inspiration, part comedic therapy, always by my side.*

## Acknowledgments

To Ellen – thank you for giving me some teaching insight.

To Nina – thank you for sharing your incredible knowledge about all things soap and for the incredible products you make at Dúagwyn Farm. You, with your brave heart and warm smile, and your babies, have brought great joy to many people.

To Brian and Guy – thank you for being my parasailing test subjects since I was too afraid of sharks to go that far out into the ocean. I love both of you!

To my editor, Deelylah Mullin - thank you for making me a better writer.

To my beta reader and all-around best woman, Sue - thank you for pushing me along.

# Chapter One

Lizbeth stared at the handle on the door, willing it to open while her freshly washed hands dripped on the ceramic tile floor. *YUCK! Don't make me touch that thing.* Near pin-straight aging auburn hair glided back and forth as she rolled her head to either shoulder, attempting to relieve the tension in her neck.

Few things grossed her out more than touching a public bathroom door handle without benefit of protection. *Something? Anything? Paper towel? Shirt sleeve?* Yet, there she stood, on a hot June day, wearing a tank top and shorts, inside a truck stop ladies' room in Somewhere, North Carolina with nothing to prevent scads of revolting germs from touching her.

Just as she was about to give up, with her hand a fraction of an inch from the worn brass, the door popped open, nearly striking her in the head. Lizbeth looked to the ceiling, laughing out loud at herself. *Idiot. Trapping yourself in here.* With no explanation to the confused looking stranger holding the door for her, Lizbeth bolted for the front of the store and the relative germ-free safety of the car.

"Hey Liz, you want a snack?" she heard her travelling companion, Carolee, shout.

Turning around to see the other woman's devious grin while pointing to an open countertop container of unwrapped donuts, Lizbeth rolled her eyes, knowing she was being teased. With over twenty years of teaching together, her friends knew she wouldn't eat anything left out for people to man-handle.

"You're a jerk," she jokingly admonished Carolee. "I'll wait outside."

Crossing the parking lot quickly, Lizbeth approached the other woman she was travelling with. "Seriously, Amy. How did you two talk me into this?"

The younger woman shrugged her shoulders. "Believe me, we were very surprised that you agreed. Happy, but surprised." The hot southern sun played peek-a-boo with the gold flecks in her tow-head blonde hair. "What's the problem?"

Before Liz could answer, the ever-dramatic voice of Carolee was behind her. "Oh, nothing. Ms. Germ-a-phobe here had to use a public toilet."

Amy bent over laughing in response. "Really, Lizbeth? You're freaked out over a little bathroom break?" Amy's flaxen pony tail swished back and forth across her shoulders. "It's better than wetting your pants. Or, for cripes sake, it's a hell of a lot better than you peeing in my back seat." She motioned for her companions to get in the car. "Now, load up ladies. We're burning daylight while we're standing here yacking."

After nearly two decades with side-by-side classrooms, Lizbeth was unphased by Amy's bossiness. Not only was she a taskmaster with her students, but Amy was the only female in a large family of construction workers. Lizbeth knew from her stories that growing up in Amy's world you either took control or got trampled on the way to the dinner table.

Returning to the highway, Amy and Carolee chatted between themselves about problems they had each experienced during the just-ended school year. Not wanting to discuss the personal issues of any students, Lizbeth reclined her seat and pulled a blanket over her head, feigning fatigue and hoping the rhythmic sound of the road would put her to sleep.

*Why did I agree to this trip?* She shifted in her seat, hoping to drive the nagging question away. *It's simple. Since Jim died, you've had no life. If you're going to be hot and sweaty all summer, the ocean is much preferable to inner-city Albany. Besides, it might be fun!* On that last thought, she took a deep, cleansing breath and let it out slowly. With about two hours to their destination, a quick nap appealed to her.

"REALLY? WHO THINKS OF THESE NAMES?" Lizbeth grumbled to her companions as they crossed the sweltering black asphalt parking lot of the *Piggly Wiggly*. "And why did we drive all the way down here for this store? We must have passed ten—much bigger—supermarkets since we left the house."

In her peripheral vision, Lizbeth saw Carolee's dramatic shrug. Turning to look, she noticed the brunette's face pinking up. "Why Carolee, you're blushing. Is there something you want to tell us about this little ol' store?"

"Nope." Tight lipped, Carolee continued walking.

"You've been here before, haven't you?" Amy poked Carolee's thick arm. "Fess up!"

"Nope."

"Carolee!" Amy had stopped walking. "I know you're up to something."

"Nope."

Lizbeth roared with laughter. "Come on. How many years of secondary education to be a teacher and that's all you've got? Single syllable slang?"

Carolee was almost to the front door when she shouted back at them. "Yep." Giggling, she stepped inside the store and into the arms of a tanned adonis, leaving her shocked companions to gape in the blistering South Carolina sun.

Amy's pony tail danced furiously as she pivoted to face Lizbeth. "Did you just see that? I mean. I mean, really Liz. Did you know about this?"

Holding up her hands, Lizbeth was struggling to contain her mirth. "Why are you asking me? She's your drinking buddy."

Amy tipped her head, accentuating the look of disbelief, her eyes wide and blinking. "I. Uh. Wait. No, I don't think she's ever said anything about a man-friend down here."

Liz wrapped her arm around the younger woman's shoulder, steering her into what she hoped was an air-conditioned oasis. "Well, apparently she's been withholding a rather interesting secret." Pointing to the unexpected couple, Liz continued needling her. "See that tongue dancing? I think they've done this before."

Leaving Amy to digest the news, Lizbeth grabbed a shopping cart. "Come, chick," she pulled Amy back to reality. "We know most of the stuff on the list. Carolee will find us when she's ready." Waving to their friend, Liz led Amy to start browsing through the foreign store, pointing to various unique items and brands they couldn't buy in the Northeast.

Half an hour later, when Liz saw Carolee approaching, she grabbed Amy before the blonde woman could pounce. "Hey, give her space. She'll tell us when she's ready."

Practically growling under her breath, Amy pulled away from the hand Liz had placed on her shoulder. "Okay. I'll try."

Older than either of them by nearly ten years, Lizbeth frequently found herself refereeing between the friends. "You two chat while I head over to see what the meat selection is like." Without waiting for an answer, she slipped Amy's hand off the shopping cart and walked away with it.

Rounding the corner, she took a quick look at the two women who were now hugging. Amy tipped her head back in robust laughter when Carolee's dimples deepened as a huge smile spread across her face. Shaking her head, Liz often thought the two had a friendship that bordered on sibling rivalry.

Lizbeth practically fell ass-over-teakettle into her own cart from the jolt of running into another shopper. "Oh, shit. Excuse me!" She felt the heat of embarrassment rushing up her neck and flooding her cheeks. *Oh my!* She found herself staring into a pair of slate blue eyes—ones with a teasing twinkle. *Say something, Liz.* She darted around the cart, reaching her hand out to the delectable stranger.

"I am so sorry. Did I hurt you?"

Laughter rumbled from his chest in a deep vibrato as the lines around his eyes accented their color. "No, I'm okay. Really." He wrapped his hand around her extended one. "I'm Beau Landry."

His touch was some sort of unspoken cliché as uncontrollable need tingled her hand. Liz was sure he had one of those hidden hand buzzers she had played with in her youth. "Lizbeth Spensor." She was pretty sure she'd said her name.

"How pretty and unique." His southern accent warmed her.

As he continued to hold her hand, Liz felt a flutter in her groin. She shivered slightly, pulling away from his magical grasp. "Thank you. I— I get that a lot." She shook her head slightly. "I mean, people mention that my name is different. And they often try to correct me."

Beau laughed again, this time stretching his arms over his head, pulling his light cotton shirt up enough to show Lizbeth a well-tanned abdomen with swirling tawny hair that disappeared into the elastic waist band of a pair of faded swim trunks.

*Sweet Josephine!* She had to get away from this looker before Amy and Carolee found *her* blushing like a teenager. Stepping back to the handle of her shopping cart, Liz kept her eyes averted.

"Is it something I said?"

His question drew her back in as an unbidden grin spread across her flaming cheeks. "No, not at all. It's just that I need to catch up with my friends." When she raised her eyes to his, she saw him give her a slight nod.

"Blonde with a pony tail and a curly brunette?"

Lizbeth felt her shoulders sag when she realized what he would say next.

"I think they're standing right behind you." His hands slid into unseen pockets in his trunks, pulling his shirt tight across his chest. Through the thin material, Liz admired a dusting of more hair on his solid pecs.

Knowing her travelling companions would be admiring him as well, she decided to tackle them head on. Momentarily stepping to one side of the cart, Lizbeth made a big, sweeping gesture. "Amy. Carolee. Meet Beau." Pulling on the handle to lead her friends away from the enticing draw of his eyes, Liz tried to move. "Okay ladies, nothing to see here. Let's finish our shopping." But Amy's firm grip trapped her.

"Liz, something to tell us?" The blonde's voice seemed to fill the *Piggly Wiggly*.

"Nope." Her single answer set all three of them into a round of giggles. After a minute of enjoying the sweet sound of her own laughter, Lizbeth turned to her new acquaintance. "Gosh, that was rude of us." Another giggle squeaked past her lips as she extended her hand. "It was a pleasure meeting you."

This time Amy and Carolee stepped aside and allowed Liz to move the cart to the front of the store, whispering between themselves. And while Lizbeth knew her friends were about to tease her brutally, she couldn't help but smile to herself as she felt the sensual gaze of Beau Landry pinned to her derriere as she walked away.

AFTER SEVERAL BLOCKS OF SILENCE, Carolee finally spoke. "I'll tell you about mine if you spill first." She turned in her seat to look at Liz.

"What's to tell? I wasn't paying attention going around a corner and crashed into him." Lizbeth shrugged and went back to looking out the window. "When do you two begin teaching?"

"Monday. We've got tomorrow to find the school and hit the beach." Liz caught Amy's gaze in the rearview mirror when she answered.

"Wait a minute. Don't you change the subject Lizbeth Spensor." Carolee put her hand on Amy's shoulder in a full pivot to challenge Liz. "That ever-so-sexy Beau couldn't take his eyes off you. And…" Carolee drew out her point, "you were blushing like a naughty teenager."

"Agreed. He was good looking. But I don't think I was blushing." Liz decided that flat-out denial was the best way to handle things. "Handsome men are the proverbial dime a dozen, Carolee. Especially in the south where a good tan and that sugary sweet accent can improve anyone's appeal. Now, tell us about your squeeze."

"No, we're still talking about yours."

"Okay, you two. That's enough. You are adults, right?" Carolee spun in her seatbelt to face forward, her lower lip pooched out in an adolescent pout as Amy pointed at her. "Check that map on your phone so I don't miss the turn off 17."

Lizbeth wanted to hug Amy for interrupting the questioning, but instead she focused on the scenery, trying to memorize the way to their temporary home.

AS SUNSET STARTED CREEPING into the back yard, Lizbeth finished making the queen-sized bed in her room and then flopped down on it. Hugging the pillow, she took in a deep breath, reveling in the familiar scent of her own linen and allowing herself to relax. She was willing to admit exhaustion after the marathon twelve-hour drive, unpacking, grocery shopping and then cooking dinner. She had volunteered for KP duty for the first week while Amy and Carolee settled into their teaching jobs. Both women were working toward an Advanced Graduate Certificate in TESOL (Teaching English to Speakers of Other Languages) and needed to complete unpaid field work teaching English as a New Language—ENL—and American History to recent immigrants as part of their required credits. Since their home school expected to begin a new ENL program, both Amy and Carolee wanted in on the ground floor, helping new immigrants and, coincidentally, boosting their salaries. With three devastating hurricanes last summer in the Atlantic Ocean, there was no shortage of people escaping their island paradises to settle on the mainland USA, even as far north as Albany, New York.

Amy and Carolee were in their early forties and had well over ten more years to work, any bump they were able to get in their salaries and subsequent pension would serve them well. But Liz was in a different world. At fifty-two years of age, she was in the enviable position of already reaching thirty years of working at the school. As a municipal employee in New York state, that was an important goal, the brass ring of service credits. The money was locked in and her financial future was solid; the only snag was that she couldn't begin collecting her pension until she turned fifty-five. In truth, she could relocate to Bali Bali and teach sand sculpture classes to tourists for the next three years—an idea that was most enticing on the days when she was trudging through two-foot deep snow from a Nor' Easter. Though she didn't need the credentials, when Amy and Carolee signed up for the experience, Liz agreed to be a substitute if either of her friends required a day off.

Standing from the bed, Lizbeth admonished herself, "Okay. Ol' Mother Hubbard, go check on those two before you pass out." Childless, she wasn't sure where her maternal instinct was coming from. Chuckling, she crossed the kitchen and dining room to find her temporary roommates on the screened-in porch, surrounded by text books, lesson plans, and pads of paper. "I can see you guys have this under control. I'm going to bed."

"Wait, Liz…" Amy's voice grabbed Lizbeth as she

turned to leave. "Bed? It's not even nine o'clock. You'll be up before dawn. Have a glass of wine with us."

"Sorry, girls. I've got the SUV version of jet lag." She looked into the backyard, catching a small red squirrel scurrying under the neatly trimmed privet hedge. "And if I'm up that early, maybe I'll go for a run and learn about our new town. Good night." She tilted her head to each of them and left.

In the privacy of the bathroom in her spacious first floor bedroom, Liz stripped off her clothes and stepped into the shower. The crisp temperature of the tile floor shot up her body, causing her nipples to harden from the chill. She folded her arms across her ribs, supporting her generous breasts as the cascading water turned hot, quieting the goose bumps. After a few moments, Liz released her girls to reach for the shampoo. Massaging her scalp, she let the lavender scent wrap her in familiar peace-fulness. Ever since she was a child, this particular bouquet reminded her of the many hours she had spent dozing in the arms of her maternal grandmother. Though she was a fierce woman who had scared many a child in her own classroom, Gertrude Kennedy's ample bosom had been sweet comfort for baby Lizbeth.

Once she rinsed her hair of the shampoo and applied conditioner, Liz grabbed the goats' milk soap from the ceramic dish molded into the shower wall. Holding it under the stream of water, she rolled the bar in her hands a minute, developing a riot of frothy softness, thinking about the day she discovered Nina and her Nigerian Dwarf goats at Dúagwyn Farm.

*During the first spring break after her husband's death, Lizbeth found herself wrapped in a perpetual cloak of sadness, unable to leave her house for days. When she realized she was out of milk and bread, she bundled up on a cold and soggy March day and made her way to* the local co-op, her preferred grocery store. As she entered the market she was greeted by the various scents of natural herbs and spices as she reached for a canvas tote. Straightening up, she faced a massive bulletin board just inches from her face, layered with paper flyers. She took a step backward, allowing her eyes to focus on the assorted typeset when they were drawn to a picture of what appeared to be a baby black-and-white goat with the single line: Find us on AirBnB!

The image of the baby goat stayed with Liz as she picked up a few staples, drove back to her house, and hunkered down with the unorthodox meal of cinnamon toast and chocolate pudding. Still feeling miserable, and a bit full, Lizbeth broke out her laptop to find the goats. When she finally landed on the correct page she fell in love with a gorgeous kid with a coal black nose, dark eyes surrounded by a black mask and a giant white stripe running from the edge of its nostrils over the top of its head and a headline that said BOTTLE FEED BABY GOATS!

The next day, Liz found herself in the wooded hills of Eastern Rensselaer County holding a fourteen hour-old kid in her lap as it suckled the warm bottle of milk she offered, fighting tears of loneliness as she absorbed the precious new life. Since Dúagwyn Farm wasn't your traditional B-n-B, Lizbeth didn't spend the night there. Instead, for the next four days of her vacation, she made the twenty-mile trip each morning to help feed the goats and then clean their pens. Leaving after she'd given several kids their noon-time bottle, she felt herself smiling for the first time in months as she drove slowly along the curved country road.

Overwhelmed with new emotion, Liz pulled into the gravel entry to a hayfield. Staring at the patches of brown dirt peeking out from a thin layer of snow, tears streamed down her cheeks when she realized that she could still be happy, even though Jim was gone from her life. Leaning her head back, she covered her wet face with her hands. Liz took a deep breath, drawing in the tender smell of lanolin that lingered from holding the baby goats. "Thank you, Nina—and your goats. You've given me much needed joy."

Well over a year since her first goat experience, Liz found that the rich scent of the soap always made her smile. Not only had she survived the worst time of her life, but she'd learned to move on. To be happy without guilt. And, she'd returned to feed new babies during the next kidding season.

With her back to the hot spray, Lizbeth ran the silken bubbles over her neck and shoulders, and then down her breasts. Cupping them one at a time to rid herself of the traces of sweat she'd felt run down her ribs earlier, Liz felt a hot jolt in her abdomen as her fingers rubbed the creamy soap across each nipple.

*Oh! Where did that come from? I was thinking of sweet baby goats!* She leaned her head back, so the pulsating jets could sluice away the conditioner and pepper her cheeks with a mini-facial. She took another moment to enjoy the warmth on her face before turning in the water to finish her minis-trations. Squatting slightly, she slid her soapy hand between her thighs, causing a surge of heat she hadn't felt in over two years—since the night before her husband died.

"Whoa." Liz half-laughed as she leaned against the shower wall. "What is up with this southern water?" She let the shower envelope her while waiting for her mound to stop throbbing. "Note to self: your lady parts are done with widowhood." Turning the single handle to OFF, Liz stood a moment while little rivulets ran down her legs, then stepped out, onto a fleece-covered foam mat—another item which had travelled with her.

A few minutes later, with her mouth fresh from pepper-mint paste and her limbs coated with almond shea butter, Lizbeth slipped her naked body into the freshly made bed. Reaching for a book on the nightstand, she realized she was too tired to read and shut off the light. Snuggling into her cocoon, vignettes from the long day popped into her mind; the rising sun as they drove through New Jersey, along with countless fast food restaurants and truck stops through Maryland and Virginia. That silly name on the grocery store, and…those eyes. That smile. That sexy southern voice. Beau Landry filled Lizbeth's sleepy head as she drifted off with a content mumble, "Mmmmm."

## Chapter Two

Skirting around some shells, Beau felt the wet sand give slightly under his weight as he stepped into the retreating wave. He loved being up while most of the world still slept —an easy thing to accomplish in a tourist mecca like Myrtle Beach, where people partied late into the night at beachside tiki bars. Having spent many years nursing a rum-induced mid-morning hangover, these days Beau preferred his day to start early, with a clear head.

He had finished most of his eight-mile beach run with just the ambient glow of countless high-rise condos to guide him. Heading north to Cherry Grove, he slowed to a walk and gazed at the sky as the colors fluctuated. The steely gray-blue gave way to a pinkish-orange glow on the horizon. Entranced as the sun made its debut at the Earth's edge, Beau lost track of his surroundings. Without thinking, he backed up several feet from the water, inadvertently stepping into the path of another person, knocking them to the ground.

Spinning around to apologize, the words froze in his throat when he extended a hand to his innocent victim. He shook his head trying to clear his vision in the misty light, but the instant she touched his proffered help, Beau knew it was her. "It seems we've bumped into each other again. Are you okay?" Watching her eyes light up with recognition, he felt the smile cross his face. *Good lord she's even better looking than I remembered.* Beau released her hand as soon as she was standing. "Lizbeth, correct?"

"Yes, it is. Is this a meeting of coincidence or are you stalking me?" He saw her eyes spark with challenge as she dusted the sand from her red nylon running shorts.

"Believe me, pure coincidence. Though I can't say that I'm disappointed." He was rewarded with a light blush. "How long have you been running?"

"About twenty minutes."

"No, I mean, how long have you been a runner?"

"Oh. Most of my life. I took it up in high school and haven't stopped." She shook her head with a deep and hearty laugh. "And we don't need to discuss how long ago *that* was."

Beau loved this woman's clarity, her laugh, and her self-deprecating humor.

"Hey, listen, I've got to finish my run before it gets too hot. Thanks, uh, for helping me up."

He panicked when he saw Lizbeth walk a few steps away from him. "Wait." He felt like the word barked at her. "Look, my house is just up the beach. Why don't you stop for coffee on the way back?" He saw her focus on the houses over his shoulder. "The yellow one with the green shutters."

Backing up a few more steps, she shook her head. "I'll be at least another half an hour. Maybe next time."

"I don't mind. And I won't even take a shower, so we can both be sweaty sitting on the porch. It's not a commitment, it's just coffee." He watched her try not to laugh as he held his hands up in mock surrender.

"Okay, but just one cup. I can't stay long." She nodded to him and then started off with the hop common to runners, setting a pace as her long, muscular legs carried her particularly sexy ass away from him.

As she faded in the distance, Beau realized she hadn't said his name. No wonder she was hesitant about having coffee. She probably thought he was some odd duck or pervert with a penchant for luring women into his home for nefarious reasons. "Jesus, Landry. Maybe it's just that she's immune to your charms. You *are* getting a little long in the tooth." Laughing, he broke into a jog to make quick work of getting to his house. He had every intention of being on the porch with a full pot of coffee and the morning paper when she returned.

HE TRIED to appear nonchalant when he saw her slow to a walk, holding the newsprint as if he were reading it. Truthfully, he'd been watching her progress up the beach toward him with her even stride. The rhythmic rocking of her hips from those powerful legs had his mind creating blush-worthy images and starting trouble in his lightweight running shorts.

She stopped at the bottom of the porch staircase. Propping her right foot up two steps, she leaned into the first leg, then the second, stretching her quads and glutes. A moment later she stood before him and accepted his hand shake as he rose in greeting. Beau saw beads of sweat running down her neck and getting lost in the tempting curves hidden inside her jersey. For a split second, he thought of how soft and salty her breasts would be right now if he were able to lick and nibble them.

"Beau?" Her voice brought him back to reality. "My eyes are up here." Though chastising him, her smile was friendly.

"Sorry. I. Uh." He pulled out a chair. "Here, please sit." Feeling like an awkward teenager, he filled the second coffee cup on the table and pointed toward the condiments. "Please, help yourself."

"Thanks. Black is fine."

"You do realize there's an unwritten rule in the south that you must use an inordinate quantity of cream and sugar in your coffee, right?"

She pursed her lips as he spoke.

"And it's against the law to drink your iced tea unless it's got so much sugar in it that your spoon stands up. It's part of living here in South Carolina."

"Well, since I'm not interested in type 2 diabetes, then, it's lucky for me that I live in the northeast."

Beau liked the sass he heard in her tone of voice. This was no southern belle and he found her delightfully refreshing. His deep laughter caused her to grin, showing a single dimple on her right cheek.

"Darlin', you may enjoy your coffee any way you'd like. Just as long as you spend a few minutes with me." He nodded to her as she took a deep swallow.

"Mmmm. Nice and rich."

"Well, since most of us destroy it with the aforementioned cream and sugar, it needs to be robust enough to still taste like coffee. I should probably be offering you water since you just came back from a run."

"I'm okay."

"Lizbeth, what brings you to South Carolina? Vacation?" He watched her over his own cup.

"Not really. But sort of."

"You mean you're not sure?" Beau shook his head in confusion but kept his eyes on hers.

"I travelled with friends. They're teachers." She set her cup on the table. "Well, we're all teachers. They are working on a special assignment to get more credits, but I'm not."

"So then, you're on vacation."

"I agreed to be their back up in case either of them needs a day off. They're teaching ENL and American History. While I'm a little weak in the language arts, I'm strong with the history so I can fill in whenever they need me."

Beau tipped his head. "ENL?"

"Oh, sorry. My life tends towards acronym hell. ENL is English as a New Language. At home I teach in a public school that's in a sanctuary city. Many of our students arrive with no understanding of the English language."

"Is Myrtle Beach a sanctuary city?"

"I have no idea. But, with the rash of hurricanes in the Atlantic, you have a high-volume of non-English speaking immigrants here. Apparently, there's a need because they were recruiting teachers from across the nation."

"Where is home?" Beau watched her closely to see if she considered her answer before giving it.

"Upstate New York." Lizbeth surprised him by refilling her coffee cup. "How about you? Myrtle Beach?"

"Charleston. Old Southern living."

"This seems like an odd place for a vacation, then." He felt her eyes pinned to him.

"It's a long story. Besides, I'm working. With technology, I can do that from just about anywhere."

Liz set down her freshly filled cup, stood up, and

stepped away from the table. "I have to go. My roommates will be worried."

She started down the stairs before Beau could stop her.

On the third step, she turned to him. "Thanks for the coffee. Take care." With a wave, she finished the remaining steps at a jog and headed up beach.

"That was odd. I wonder what I said." Beau watched her retreating figure, taking note of the public crossway where she left the sand. He considered hopping in his car to see if he could find her, but that seemed too stalkerish. He'd already run into her twice in two days—she must live around this neighborhood, somewhere.

Deep in thought over what might have triggered Lizbeth's hasty dash, Beau didn't realize that the phone had rung until his housekeeper stepped out onto the porch.

"Mr. Landry, it's your father."

*Oh, this can't be good. What's he have to say that he's calling this early on a Sunday morning?* "Thank you, Belle." He nodded politely to the older woman, waiting for her to return to the airconditioned house before speaking to his progenitor.

"Hello, Pop. What's on your mind?" Beau leaned heavily on his elbows, cradling his head in one hand while the other held the phone to his ear.

"You're needed in Charleston this week." So typical of his father. No greeting, no pretense of warmth. Just direct business.

"What for? I'm handling all of the account work from here."

"Quite frankly, Beauregard, I want you to meet with me and the head counsel of the company. This entire sordid affair has put much of our investment at risk." Even though his father sounded tired, Beau couldn't suppress the guttural reaction he had to his father using his given name.

20

"Do you have something scheduled for tomorrow?" Beau asked knowing it would only take him a few hours to travel to his home town.

"Yes, nine o'clock. Can you make that?"

"I'll be there. Bye, Pop." He severed the connection before his father could lecture him.

In Beau's opinion, there was no sordid affair. Just a gold-digging woman who claimed he was the father of her unborn child. Unfortunately, she was doing a fair amount of squawking and the local media were thrilled to have the gossip for front page news. For his part, Beau had decided that getting out of town until the juiciest part settled down was the best way to handle things. Based upon his father's phone call, the storm had not yet passed—despite his having been gone almost a month.

"Pain in the ass." Beau slapped the table as he got out of the chair. Grabbing the phone, he went into the house to take a shower. If he timed it right, he could reach Charleston about the same time most of his neighbors would be in church. With any luck, he'd be inside his own house without anyone catching sight of him.

WHEN BEAU WALKED through the front door of M.L. Incorporated, he felt the pressure crushing the air out of his lungs. Years before, he had moved his portion of the business to a different location because working in the home offices had been stifling. With his father's stern hand and unrelenting rules, it was impossible to feel like his own man. Even at forty-eight, Beau carried a sense of fore-boding for the lecture he expected from his father. Nodding to the receptionist, he started down the long hallway to his father's office suite. Quietly, he turned the gold filigree handle and stepped through the deep red mahogany doorway.

"Good morning, Mr. Landry." A perfectly coiffed woman addressed him with a soft drawl, causing Beau to look around the carpeted office to see if his father was there. When his gaze returned to the woman, he noticed a light blush infuse her delicate neck. Appearing at the edge of a soft pink chenille sweater, it flowered up under a string of pearls to her cheeks.

"I'm sorry, we've not met." Beau extended his hand to the southern beauty. Having spent the past month in the touristy area of Myrtle Beach, he discovered that he missed the gentility of Charleston. "I'm Beau Landry."

"I know. I've seen your pictures. Ivy. Ivy Dolan." She left her manicured hand in his grasp for a moment longer than true propriety dictated.

Beau stepped back from her desk. "You must be new here." He saw her start to smile at his obvious statement. "I have a nine o'clock appointment with the elder Mr. Landry."

"Yes sir, you can go right in." She pointed at a door about two feet away from her desk.

"Thank you." Beau nodded to her, taking note of what appeared to be a gleam in her eye. He assumed Ivy Dolan had entertained herself with the Charleston media storm. So much for southern refinement.

After closing the door to his father's private office, Beau turned to face Montgomery Landry. Eighth generation Charleston business man, whose once towering frame was now slightly stooped as he stood to shake his son's hand.

"Beauregard, it's good to see you." Despite his age, the older Landry's handshake was still firm.

"Hi, Pop. It's nice to be here." Beau hoped his father wouldn't see through the obvious lie.

"Son, this is our new chief counsel. James Azure." Beau turned to the middle-aged man sitting at an imposing oak table on the left side of the room. As the attorney stood to greet him, Beau took note of the expensive suit covering his generous girth.

"Mr. Azure, Beau Landry." He swallowed the man's extended hand with his own, giving him a good strong pump.

When his father joined the two younger men at the table, Beau decided a proactive approach was better than being reactive to any lecture that might be coming. "Pop, I don't know why you're referring to my brief relationship with Josie Fitch as a sordid affair—we are both consenting adults. I figured out pretty quickly that she was far more attracted to my money than to me."

"Son, she is threatening to file a lawsuit against M.L. Incorporated, Southerner's Folly Incorporated, and you individually."

"Based upon what?" Beau grabbed the engraved wooden arm rests of the conference chair he sat in, effectively anchoring himself so that he didn't launch and pace the office.

"She claims that you are the father of her unborn child." Beau felt his father's eyes pin him. "Are you?"

"No." It was all he could manage through clenched teeth. This was a conversation that could have been held privately between father and son. But, Montgomery Landry—always the business man first and father second—had elected to have it in front of a witness. Beau felt his left eye twitch as a smirk spread from one cheek to the other.

"Beauregard, you seem to think this is a comical matter."

"No, Pop. No, I don't." He took a deep breath before

continuing. "I'm not sure why this chat required me to drive three hours just for you to bring up my personal life with a stranger in the room."

"James is no stranger," Montgomery boomed at his son.

"Well, he is to me." Beau stood up and crossed to the large bank of windows facing the Charleston Harbor. As he watched a large speedboat cut across the water, he desperately wished he were on it instead of being trapped in a room with his domineering parent and an odious attorney. *I guess it's time to give it to him straight.* Turning back to face the two men, Beau knew his father would regret what he was about to hear.

"Pop. There is absolutely no way in hell that I can be the father of her child." He waited for his father to inter-rupt but Montgomery Landry sat quietly with his hands folded on the table in front of him. "About a year after Carli's mother died, I started dating a woman from up in Mt. Pleasant. She thought I should introduce her to Carli and do things together as a group, so my little girl would have a female figure around her. I ignored the suggestion for a month or two, and just kept going up to see her instead of inviting her down. It might not have been very gentlemanly of me, but the more she pushed me, the less I liked her, except for the sex."

Beau turned back to looking at the water before contin-uing. "Then, one day she tells me she's pregnant. When I got done panicking, I decided that I didn't want her around my daughter. I waited a week or two and told her I wanted her to have a paternity test. At first, she refused. Then she confessed to all of it being a lie."

He stared at the deep greenish-blue of the harbor, nervously jiggling some change in his pocket before returning to the table. Without sitting, he looked his father in the eye. "Pop, I decided then that I would never wonder about another child or be accused again, so I had a vasectomy right after that. And once a year I go to my doctor to have tests done to make sure there aren't any swimmers making their way upstream." Beau watched his father's jaw tighten under his aging skin, his pulse throbbing rapidly in his neck as his eyes turned to ice.

"How dare you commit to such a life-altering event without my knowledge." His father's hands were now flat on the table as the man pushed himself up to stand. "You are my only son. And now…now you tell me there is no one to carry on the Landry name. That there will be no tenth generation of the Landry family?"

With his temper raging through him, Beau struggled not to launch a full verbal assault on his father—especially in front of the attorney. "Carli is the tenth generation."

"Oh, stop it. She's a girl."

"No, Pop. She's a woman. And a really bright one who graduated Magna Cum Laude from Clemson with her MBA. And she's damn good at the work she does at Southerner's Folly. Maybe you should try to get to know her." Beau knew he was shouting but he was beyond caring. "Just because she doesn't have a pair of balls and didn't go to The Citadel doesn't make her any less a Landry."

Montgomery Landry sat heavily in the chair, unwilling to meet his son's eyes, further triggering Beau's temper—which caused him to spin toward the attorney. "Mr. Azure. Your time would be well-spent telling Ms. Fitch that if she doesn't make a public retraction of all her salacious lies, that she will be sued by M.L. Incorporated, Southerner's Folly Incorporated, and me as an individual."

Beau crossed the luxurious cream carpeting to the door, placing his hand on the detailed gold knob. "Gentlemen, I'm leaving now. I will be returning to Myrtle Beach after a few hours at the Folly." Slowly he turned the handle without opening the massive door. "And Pop? Maybe next time you will give me the courtesy of privacy when you have something to say to me."

Wrapped in a cloak of raw indignation, Beau left the halls of his family's empire without speaking to anyone. As he drove the length of Meeting Street, he knew he wasn't going over to his own arm of the company, Southerner's Folly. Instead, he jumped on the interstate at first chance, playing with the rack and pinion steering of his Mercedes Benz as the unmistakable saxophone work of John Coltrane warmed his heart and thoughts of a long-legged runner filled his mind.

# Chapter Three

"Admit it, you're avoiding the beach," Amy said as she sat on the back porch with the Sunday paper and Lizbeth. "But we're going today."

"I'm not avoiding it. I've found other places to run, that's all." Liz regretted, if only briefly, telling Amy about her encounter with Beau Landry the week before.

"Look, I don't usually insert myself into your life—"

"Why start now?" Lizbeth interrupted her friend in mid-sentence.

"Why?" Amy dropped the paper to her lap. "For several reasons, Lizbeth. For starters, we are friends. And, despite our age gap, I truly love and respect our friendship." She paused for a swallow of coffee. "And, I've watched your broken heart overwhelm your life with sadness since Jim died. But *you* didn't die. It's been over two years. I want to hear you laugh again, Liz. You're a beautiful, smart, and sexy woman. And, you're only fifty-two. That's not old. It's time for you to get back in the game of life rather than watching from the sidelines. And, by the way, that guy is one hot number."

Lizbeth was silent, digesting what Amy had said. Truly, in that moment she couldn't decide if she felt proud that her friend had spoken her mind or trampled by the run-on attack. She stared across the backyard. The morning dew still lingered on the grass in the shaded area under an enormous live oak tree. Given the diameter of its trunk, she wondered how old the majestic monster was. When she heard Amy take a deep breath, Liz held up her hand to stop any additional lecture while she collected her thoughts.

"You don't understand, Amy. I'm not sure I know how to—as you put it—get back in the game." Standing, Lizbeth crossed the porch to lean on the railing before looking at Amy. "I was with the same man for thirty years. I didn't have to work on titillating conversation, it just happened, mostly 'cause Jim was a talker. And, he thought of the places we'd travel to, restaurants we'd frequent."

She saw her friend's eyes widen with surprise at this confession.

"Maybe I never told you, but Jim was a bully. Always telling me that he was superior, in every way. IQ, family wealth, athletics." Liz took a deep breath before continuing. "I was so young and naïve that I didn't consider pushing back. Then, when the doctor said I'd never have children…" She paused a moment, trying to control the sad shake she felt in her voice. "Basically, I slipped into a deep grieving sadness. And the Catholic guilt wouldn't let me divorce him. I gave up and left him in charge over just about everything in my life."

"I don't know what to say. The way you take over things at work, I always thought you were the dominant one in the Spensor household."

"Ha, ha, ha!" Lizbeth couldn't contain her sudden outburst. "That's because he wasn't at the school to control me." She turned away when she felt the unwelcome, but all too familiar, tears fill her eyes. It was so difficult to discuss her late husband and what was essentially an unhappy marriage. "I won't let anyone have that power over me ever again."

Liz heard Amy's chair move just moments before she felt the younger woman's arms wrap her in a sturdy embrace. "How about we start with you learning to have fun first?"

She let the warmth of Amy's friendship sooth her another moment before responding. "I'd like that. Can we start with the Parasail Winery tour before the beach?"

LONG BEFORE THAT morning's discussion with Amy, Liz had forced herself to step out of her proverbial safety zone box. Each day, after her roommates left, she would hop on her bicycle and explore the area to one side, or the other, of Route 17. During the first week in Myrtle Beach, on South Ocean Boulevard, she found countless rental properties, condominiums, and massive houses. Each time she thought she'd memorized the location of one, she stumbled upon yet another *South Shore, Dune Scape, Ocean Edge, Carolina Reef, Crescent Shores, Castaway Beach* or *Crescent Beach*. The names and soft Williamsburg paint schemes blended together as they melted into the sand.

"Good lord, what if you came home drunk. How would you know which house you were staying in?" Liz mumbled to herself while waiting for the opportunity to cross the busy street.

Once heading north again, she realized she was happy. Running around by herself had been one way of working on some of her fears without discussing it with Amy or

Carolee. For most of her life, people had been telling her where she would go and how to get there. First her parents, then her late husband. Liz smiled as she realized the power of those decisions belonged to her, and her alone. Before she left the house on the first day, she'd locked the address in the map on her phone and tucked it into her back pocket. After that, she was free to roam, knowing her electronic breadcrumbs would get her home. Every day she set out to discover as much of the city as she could on her bicycle—in effect, conquering this strange new place. And, for as simple as that sounded, it made her feel good.

Lizbeth thought about her newfound independence while squeezed in the back seat of a local ride-share car when she and her friends set out for an early afternoon playdate involving wine. Since none of them were assigned to be the designated driver, Liz was sure Amy and Carolee would be nursing a hangover when they faced their classrooms in the morning. As for herself, it didn't matter if she drank enough to drown a horse, she didn't have to work the next day. The thought occurred to her as all three were walking into the massive, yet classy, wooden structure and she couldn't resist laughing out loud.

"Something I said, Lizbeth?" Carolee placed her hand on Liz's right arm.

"Nope. Just thinking about how drunk you two are going to get today. And, that I won't care tomorrow morning because I'll still be in bed."

"Well, it was hot out there looking at all those vines and big metal tanks." Carolee pouted as she justified the need to quench her thirst.

"We can handle our wine. Come on, Carolee. I'm parched." Full of bravado, Amy pulled her friend past a long row of high wooden ladder-back stools to pick out their seats at the tasting bar, her hand making a grand, sweeping gesture. "Mount up ladies and let the party begin."

As she settled in her perch, Lizbeth noticed that there were no clocks visible—anywhere—in the well-lit room. She understood the reasoning in a bar: if people didn't know what time it was, they were more inclined to drink and spend more money. But she thought the tasting rooms in wineries were supposed to be just that—not a gin mill, not a place where old timers escaped hated jobs or nagging wives. They were where potential customers arrived in groups to find new wines, to learn to pair wines with foods and, to laugh.

Liz had to admit it was new territory for her. She really wasn't much of a drinker, other than the occasional glass of wine that would be suggested in a high-end restaurant or champagne at a wedding. Carolee and Amy, on the other hand, were far more street knowledgeable about adult beverages. But when an attractive thirty-something man in a logo T-shirt greeted them with a smile, both of her travelling companions ceased to display any type of knowledge.

"Hi ladies, I'm Liam. Welcome to Parasail on this fine Sunday afternoon. We hope all of our products make you so happy that you feel like you can float across the ocean."

Lizbeth had to hold back her laughter when both younger women seemed to swoon at the smooth, southern accent that flowed from his lips. He placed small, stemmed glasses in front of the three ladies and then retrieved an open bottle from the shelf behind him. When his back was to them, Liz quickly picked up the glass in front of her, turning it several times before returning it to the counter. *It looks like somebody shrunk these wine glasses. Guess they don't want to serve too much.*

"Can I get you started with a very light sparkler we call Coastal Breeze?"

This time she openly giggled as her companions nodded mutely, but with wide smiles on their faces. *Geez, I should figure out a way to bottle this whole southern sweetness thing. Look at what a pair of push-overs these two have become.* Lizbeth accepted the small serving from Liam, swirling the beverage in her glass as she'd seen people do in the movies and then took a small sip. *Yum, sort of like fruity seltzer.* She watched Amy taste the champagne, surprised by how much she drank in. Liz raised the glass to her lips a second time. Deciding that she'd been too dainty with the first taste, she allowed a delightfully large amount of bubbles to fill her mouth. *Ooh, fun!* As the light flavor bounced around her taste buds, she wondered why she'd never tried wine tasting before as she finished the remaining champagne.

Placing her empty glass on the counter, Lizbeth waited for Liam to come back to her.

"Ready for your next white?"

Liz smiled and nodded silently. She watched his large hands, one flat on the bar while the other palmed a bottle with a colorful label. Once he had refreshed both Amy and Carolee's glasses, Liam told them about the type of grapes used, the year it was made, and other details Liz wrote down on the list the winery provided. Ever the teacher, she was sure that one of them would want to reference her notes later.

When they moved to the fourth round, Amy nudged her right arm. Liz looked up from her note-taking to see her friend making odd gestures with her eyebrows and tilting her head toward her.

"What is wrong with you?"

Amy's eyebrows jumped up in silent answer while her hand splayed on the bar, her index finger pointing left.

When Liz turned to see why Amy had turned into a mime, she nearly fell off the stool. *Whoa. Too much wine.* Her thoughts somersaulted when the cobalt eyes of Beau Landry found her own, a smile lighting up his face. *Again? How?* Liz's mind raced in lunatic circles trying to figure out how he had found them. For a paranoid second, she thought he had followed her. But it had been over a week since she'd been anywhere near the beach. And they didn't drive to the winery, leaving Amy's car with the deep yellow and blue New York plates inside the garage at their rental house. She thought about the driver who had  brought them to Parasail, but there was simply no way Beau could have traced three New Yorkers to one middle-aged ride share driver making some extra money on a Sunday.

"Seriously?" It was all she could think of to say.

"Um. I really am not stalking you." His smile faded with seriousness. "But, hi." He extended his hand to her.

Amy gave her arm a whack from behind, causing it to jut forward. As he received her "shake," Liz nearly gasped from the heat that traveled up her arm from his touch. *Maybe it's the wine.* "Hi." *Sweet Josephine, you sound like an idiot.* Fortunately, her friends were more in control of their wits. Amy reached in front of Liz, waving to Beau.

"Hi. We're Amy and Carolee."

"Yes, I remember meeting you in the *Piggly Wiggly*."

"Hi, nice to see you again." Carolee smiled sweetly, playing with a new southern drawl she'd developed since they arrived in South Carolina.

Beau stood up, pushed his stool in and leaned on the back. "I'll leave you ladies to your afternoon. There's room farther down the tasting bar."

"No, stay." Lizbeth wasn't sure where her voice came from or why those words had tumbled from her mouth.

"Okay, then. I will." Beau's smile returned when he

pulled his stool back up to her left side. "Where on the tasting list are you lovely ladies?"

Liz slid the paper to him and turned to her friends. With a wide-eyed look of shock and her hands facing up in question, she mouthed 'now what?' to them.

Amy leaned into her ear. "Enjoy him. He smells good!" Then, turned into a giggling pile of woman as she leaned on Carolee, causing both to sound like teenagers until Liam returned to ask if they wished to continue. "Sorry, yes." Amy sat up and faced the man she'd been drooling over for an hour. "I think we're ready for the reds now."

As he turned to select a few bottles, Lizbeth gently cradled her glass. Sniffing what remained of the light bouquet, she turned to Beau and pointed to the list. "We're here."

She watched as he lifted a large cruet from the counter and poured a small amount of water into her glass. "Rinse." He waited while she swirled the glass a few times. "You can pour it in there." He pointed to a large earthen crock next to the cruet. "You want to get rid of that sweetness from the whites before you start on the reds. If you were in a different environment, you'd get a new glass."

"Why?"

"Typically, red wines are served in a larger, more shallow glass than whites are."

"Oh." She felt herself blush. "I'm new at this."

"Really?" He leaned back. "But I thought New York had many lovely wineries."

Lizbeth couldn't help but laugh. "We probably do. But I've never been to them."

"What about your friends?"

Liz's shoulders shook with a hearty chuckle. "Honestly, I have no idea. But I've never heard them talk about it."

Beau pointed to Lizbeth's list. "Well, you appear to

have things under control so I'm just going to keep you company."

Lizbeth looked at the list, and then at Beau. *Oh Liz, big mistake. Did those eyes get bluer?* "Actually, I'm all ears if you know something about this."

This time when he reached for the list, he lightly grazed Liz's left hand, sending sparks up her arm. "Believe me, it's not complicated. White before red. Dry before sweet. And, like you're doing, keep track of which ones you like best. Wineries love it when you leave a tasting with a case full of bottles."

"Well, then." Liz raised her glass. "I say, let's move on to the reds." Turning slightly to her handsome company, Lizbeth saw Beau smile and nod discreetly to the vintner to resume the tasting.

As he splashed a small amount of cabernet into each of the glasses, Liz couldn't resist licking her lips as the light bouquet reached her nose. A deep throated chuckle from Beau added to the warmth already coursing through her from the wine. Trying for nonchalance, she tipped her head toward him. "Sir? You have something to say?"

"Oh, not really." His laugh deepened. "Just enjoying your reactions."

Liz couldn't decide if that was supposed to be mockery or a compliment, so she didn't respond. Instead, she focused on Liam and what he was saying about the present wine in her glass. But as she raised it to her lips, Liz could feel Beau watching her. Suddenly, very self-conscious about having his sizzling blue eyes on her, she accidentally took a large swallow. Unprepared for how the dry red would hit the back of her tongue, Liz drew her lips into a sudden pucker and shuddered.

"Oh. Not what I expected." She saw Beau place his glass on the bar in front of them.

35

"Try a smaller sip."

Doing as instructed, Liz raised the glass to her mouth and took in about a teaspoon's worth. But wine drinking grace still managed to allude her as she felt her shoulders twitch involuntarily as a cold shot ran down her spine.

"Oh, no." Pushing away the glass in front of her, Liz expressed her dismay at the second swallow of cabernet. "Not for me."

Beau's amusement returned as he reached across for her glass and poured the unwanted wine into the bucket. After his own followed suit, he rinsed both glasses with water.

"You might want to wait until your buddies get through the next two before trying again." Lizbeth felt her brows furrow in question at his statement. "I'm not sure your immature pallet is ready for the dry reds."

"Immature?" Without rising from her stool, she planted her hands on her hips in challenge.

"Calm yourself, Yankee. It's not an insult." He placed his hand over hers, causing a searing heat to race through her despite the rising indignation she felt. "That's how the wine industry refers to people who have just begun drinking it. Many, many people start out preferring the sweeter whites and blushes."

Liz felt a sudden chill when he lifted his hand. *Put it back. Please.*

"For some folks, it takes years before their taste buds mature enough to like dry reds."

As his honeyed accent played with her, Lizbeth lost track of why her temper had flared. *I could listen to him all day.*

About fifteen minutes later, after Amy and Carolee giggled their way through two more reds, Liam poured a small amount of wine in Liz's glass. After delicately swirling the garnet-colored beverage, Beau reached for her. Placing one hand on the glass and the other on hers, his left index finger traced the lines of wine lacing the round bowl of the glass.

"These are called legs. Much like women, some wines have better legs than others." She felt him squeeze her hand slightly to magnify the nuance of his statement. Beau nodded to the glass in her hand. "Go ahead. I think you'll like this one."

Slowly, Lizbeth raised it to her lips and took a small taste. "Hhhmmm." She couldn't resist vocalizing her pleasure at the vaguely sweet grapiness and took a longer pull from the glass. "You're right. I do like this."

Beau moved the hand that had been on hers to the back of her chair, resting on the top of the light blonde wood. "Well, Lizbeth. By time you're ready to head north, we will have turned you into a wine drinker."

*Keep the wine flowing, Sugar, and I might never leave South Carolina.* Leaning back, she felt his arm slip off the chair and rest comfortably on her shoulder. Liz turned to face him, ready to comment about the wine when she saw him gesturing to her companions.

"But, I don't know about these two." His deep laugh was directed at Amy and Carolee. "They don't seem to care about the wine spectrum. They've put away everything with gusto, whether it was dry or sweet."

Liz felt his chest rumble when he wrapped his arm around her a little tighter. *Good lord. Is it the wine or is this man full-on electric?* She didn't have time to answer her own question because Carolee picked that moment to announce that she needed to use the ladies' room. But as her short legs aimed for the floor, the nearly twelve-inch drop proved too much for her as she landed on the floor in a wine-saturated, giggling puddle.

"Oh, boy." Lizbeth vaulted for her friend, pulling her upright with Amy's help. "Looks like it's *Uber* time, ladies."

For some inexplicable reason, her statement sent both younger women into uncontrollable laughter as they wobbled in the direction of the rest rooms. Blushing with embarrassment, Liz turned to Beau and Liam. "Sorry 'bout that. I probably should have fed them before we came here."

Beau gestured to the stool she'd vacated. "Nonsense. Are you their mother or their friend?"

Liz wasn't sure where he was going with this, but she returned to her seat next to him.

"Liam will put together a case of the favorites you marked on here." He slid Lizbeth's note-laden tasting list toward the grinning younger man. "And when the dynamic duo returns from the powder room, I will drive all of you home."

Liz felt a pang of fear shoot through her. "But you've been drinking."

Beau shook his head at her. "Not really. I only had a few sips of the drier reds." Pointing to the bucket he continued, "I poured much of mine out."

"Oh." Lizbeth didn't know what to say to push back his offer. She really didn't want him to know where their house was, especially since it was only a few blocks from his. But before she was able to formulate a plausible excuse for using the ride sharing service, her inebriated room-mates returned.

"Hey, Liz. What's this?" Amy pointed to the twelve bottles of wine Liam was boxing. "Is that going home with us?"

"It sure is, ladies. And your chariot awaits." Beau leaned across the counter to pay for the wine and picked up the case. Liz saw his biceps bulge in the short sleeved linen shirt as he hoisted the box. He crossed the open floor to the exit while Amy and Carolee followed. Unsure of how the afternoon had tumbled out of her control so quickly, Lizbeth stood gaping at Liam a moment, until she heard Carolee's voice piercing the air.

"Come on, Lizzie. That hot man of yours is waiting to take us for a fun ride."

Lizbeth felt every inch of her surge with mortification as the rest of the patrons laughed at her. Nodding to Liam with the little dignity she could muster, Liz nearly loped across to the entrance, all the while making "zip it" gestures to Carolee, who was laughing uncontrollably at her own antics.

## Chapter Four

Beau knew he had overstepped his bounds with Lizbeth when she slid into the passenger's seat—especially since she was forced there by her friends, both of whom had happily jumped into the back seat of his SUV and locked their respective doors. With her lips pursed and her delicate chin jutted out, she buckled her seat belt, but refused to meet his gaze when he asked her a single question. "Ready?"

*Well, hell's bells. Maybe you should have cleared this with her before telling the younger ladies.*

"Which direction am I heading in?"

He saw Liz's jaw clench, but she didn't respond.

Catching Amy's eyes in his rearview mirror, Beau smiled.

"North on 17 until you get to the Barefoot road."

He squinted at her, unsure of what road she was referring to.

"You know, Barefoot Crossing."

"Sorry, darlin', but it doesn't sound familiar."

"Go up to North Myrtle Beach on 17, take a left on

Barefoot Resort Bridge Road by the alligator place."
Lizbeth's voice was all business.

"Thanks. That's a bit more concise." As he pulled up
to a red light, Beau looked at Liz. "Penny for your
thoughts."

He watched as a storm passed over her face, changing
her features from stern and angry to oddly amused.

"Not really. You don't want to hear it." She turned to
face him. "Not now."

For several miles of stop and go traffic, a stony silence
engulfed the air conditioned inside of Beau's Mercedes.
Even he let out a sigh of relief when a twenty-foot high
alligator came into view on the left-hand side of Route 17.

"About a tenth of a mile, take the right on to Winding
Creek." Lizbeth pointed through the windshield.

Beau drove under the posted forty-five mile-per-hour
speed limit until he saw the road signs for their turn. When
they'd gone about three hundred yards down Winding
Creek, Liz spoke up.

"See that stone wall?"

Silently, Beau nodded acknowledgement.

"You need to turn in there."

As he slowed for the turn, Beau thought about the
name of the development, Waters Edge. *Any friggin' water
here is going to be filled with 'gators. I wonder if they know that.*

"We're on Sunset. Number Ten."

Beau pulled into the driveway of a newer ranch set
back from the street and killed the engine. Unsure how to
handle the awkwardness he'd created with Lizbeth, he held
back a moment as Amy and Carolee headed into the
house, chatting loudly about the wine they intended to
drink.

*Grow a pair, Landry. You created this problem.* Shaking his
head, he emerged from the car to find Liz at the hatch-

back. *Down boy!* Beau gave a silent command to his manhood at the sight of her long, tan legs—one of which was propped on his bumper. He watched her fiddle with her sandal, willing his eyes to focus on the side of her face, or even her hands, and not the well-rounded bottom that was threatening to peek out of her shorts.

"Sorry. That clip's been bothering me for hours." Her short hair slid back into place as she stood up. With her hands on her hips and a smile on her face, Lizbeth arched her back, causing her ample bust to stretch the lavender tank top she wore.

*I know she's teasing me on purpose, but good Lord, this woman is going to kill me.* Resisting her wiles, Beau reached around her to lift the back door of the SUV and pulled out the case of wine. "Where would you like me to put this?"

"Kitchen will be fine. Thanks." Liz spun and led him to the front entrance. Once inside, she pointed to an arched doorway that opened into a bright, clean room. As soon as he set the box on the counter, the other two women showed up with glasses in hand. One pulled the cardboard case open while the second snagged a bottle.

Amy winked at Beau before leaving the room. "We're taking this tasting session out to the back porch if you care to join us."

He snuck a quick look at Lizbeth before responding. "Thanks, but I think I've already over-stayed my welcome."

"Oh, stop it. She's just prickly when she wants to be. Just between you and me, I think she's got a pretty big stick up her arse." Amy waved off his response by pointing to her friend. "But, I haven't seen her bite anybody yet and I've known her around twenty years." Amy laughed at Liz's expense and left them alone in the kitchen.

*Fix it now, Landry.* "Look, I'm sorry if I insinuated

myself into your life. But I have a good reason." He watched her eyes scan the backyard through the large window over the sink before turning to him.

"I'm listening." He thought her words were meant to encourage him, but he had a sneaking suspicion the arch of her brows told him to make it quick.

"We've only been around each other a few times. And today. Today was an accident. I had no idea that I'd run into you. But, I'm glad I did." Beau knew he was rambling, and he was afraid she'd cut him off before he could finish. "Lizbeth, I think you're beautiful. You're active, strong, and healthy. And, I'd like to get to know you better. If you'll allow it."

Her deep green eyes rounded in surprise before she spoke. "I'll show you to the door." Pivoting on one foot, she left the kitchen, leaving him no option but to follow. With her left hand on the open door, and her right one perched on her hip, she reminded Beau of the nuns that used to scare him as an elementary school child. But that was a long time ago, and this woman was not his teacher. And, she was hot. He couldn't walk away without one last attempt.

Standing less than a foot away from her, he caught a whiff of her light floral scent. He saw the color of her eyes shift from hazel to a steely gray and then back to green, revealing what he assumed were tumultuous thoughts. The late afternoon sun streaming in kissed her freshly moistened lips, causing a jolt of heat to travel through his abdomen.

Without a word of permission, Beau slid his hand around her neck and gently drew her forward, despite how rigid she held her body. His free hand cupped her jaw while his tongue traced her exceptional lips, teasing them to open. He heard his own slight moan surface when she relented. Parting her lips just slightly as her hips flexed forward, making contact with his pulsing package, her breasts scorched his chest through the light linen of his shirt. His mind dove deeper than his tongue as he thought about the things he wanted to do to this incredibly sexy woman, driving his lust to a fever pitch. Just when he thought he'd explode, he felt Lizbeth pull away.

"Um. I'm not sure what to say." She looked at her hands splayed on the front of his shirt but not at him directly.

"Say you'll have dinner with me. Tomorrow night."

"I— I promised those two that I'd be on KP duty for them." She pointed back to the kitchen.

"I think they can handle calling for take-out." He ran his thumb over the vein pulsing at the edge of her jaw. On the second pass, her breathing hitched as she leaned into his hand. "A real dinner. A real restaurant. I'll pick you up and drop you off." He cupped her jaw and lifted her chin so she was forced to look at him. "What do you say?"

Beau watched the swirling color cross her eyes again. Stepping back before she answered, the tip of her tongue passed over her lips. "Yes. I'd like that."

Leaning forward, he kissed her lightly. "Great, I'll pick you up at six." He started off the front porch but turned around. "It's a beach formal restaurant."

As she closed the door, Lizbeth gave him a half nod, half smile followed by a wink. "Got it."

As he left their neighborhood, Beau swapped out the John Coltrane CD for one from Harry Connick, Junior, smiling as the young crooner filled his head with Southern swagger.

❧❧

*WHAT JUST HAPPENED?* Lizbeth tried to slow her breathing as she leaned against the smooth, cool wood of the front door. Somewhere between arriving home  and now, she'd lost sight of the original anger Beau Landry had triggered in her and had instead turned into a hot mess.

*What a tongue. That bulge. Those pecs.* She couldn't remember the last time a kiss had turned on her libido like this. *Maybe Amy's right. Maybe I can just have hot sex with this walking package of southern comfort.*

Laughing, she pushed herself off the door and headed to the kitchen. Grabbing a stemless glass from the cupboard, and a fresh bottle from the case of wine, she joined Amy and Carolee on the back porch.

"What took so long? Did you bury him in the front yard?" Carolee started laughing at her own joke.

With no intention of letting on to what  really happened, Liz responded. "No. But I did give him the address of the school where you two are working. He'll drop by tomorrow to teach your students how to speak with a sweet accent."

Carolee laughed at Liz's response, but Amy didn't fall for the ruse. "When's your first date?"

"What are you talking about?" Liz tried to be stern with her friend.

"You're blushing like a teenage girl, Liz. So, something's up."

"It's probably the wine." Lizbeth walked to the edge of the porch, happy she had yet to sit down. "You know, it's so cool in the house, it seems a shame to heat it up by cooking. How do you feel about sandwiches for dinner?"

"Liz, between the two of us, we've had about four bottles of wine. Do you think we care?" Amy laughed at her. "We've been here almost two weeks. Don't we have any left overs?"

"Well, actually…"

"Never mind. I want peanut butter and jelly. How about you, Carolee?"

Liz turned around when she heard a chair scrape across the porch floor. She saw Carolee start to stand and then drop herself back into the chair, setting off a case of her own giggles.

"Nope, nuttin'. I just wanna go to bed."

The second time she tried to stand, Liz gave her some support. "I'll help you."

"Nope. I got this." Leaning down to Amy, Carolee planted a sloppy kiss on the blonde's cheek. Then she turned to Liz with her arms extended. "Good night, ladies." Releasing Lizbeth, the youngest of the three toddled across the porch and into the house, leaving Amy and Liz with a freshly opened bottle of wine to entertain themselves.

After they watched her disappear into the house, Amy wasted no time with her interrogation. "Spill."

Liz stalled for a moment, trying to decide if she would admit to the throbbing surge of heat Beau Landry had caused in her groin. "He asked me to go out with him."

"Whoa. Like a real date?" Placing her glass on the table, Amy leaned forward in her chair.

"Of course, like a real date. I'm not some easy gin mill pick-up, you know."

"I never suggested you were. But a few hours ago, you were pushing back on doing anything outside of this house. And I mean with me and Carolee, let alone some sexy hunk 'a burning love." Amy's voice dropped into a deep Elvis impersonation.

"Well, I have to admit that I'm out of my league, here." Liz played with her wine, pretending to enjoy the sight of the legs as it rolled in the round vessel while nervous energy threatened to make her throw up.

"What's that supposed to mean? We've been through this, Liz. You're smart and sexy. You're a mature woman who knows what she wants, has control of her world, and just happens to be horny."

"Hey!" Liz tried to protest Amy's last statement, but her friend kept needling her.

"Seriously now, how long has it been since you've gotten laid?"

"Wow. Um, I— I don't know." Liz couldn't meet her eyes. "I guess it was the night before Jim died."

Amy slapped the table. "What? You never told me that. So, you've been walking around feeling guilty all this time?"

"Well, I don't know if I'd say guilty. And why would I tell you, anyway?" Liz had never discussed such intimacies with anyone else. "Really, you have these conversations with Carolee?"

"Uh, yeah." A bubbling laugh poured from her lips. "I got news for you, our chubby friend is doing the mambo all over the beach with Mister Grocery Store Casanova."

Liz could feel her cheeks flare with embarrassment and held up her hand before Amy continued. "Please spare me the details."

"Hey, you might get some ideas."

"Well, it's not going to matter. I'm not having sex with Mr. Landry—it's just dinner."

This time Amy barked in hilarity at Lizbeth's declaration, rolling from side to side in her chair. "Oh, Liz. You are one funny bitch. Fifty bucks says you don't make it to the second date before you get a piece of him."

Incensed by the implication that her behavior would be less than circumspect, Liz shook Amy's extended hand.

"You, sister, better stop at the ATM on your way home tomorrow." Chugging down the remainder of her wine, she stood from the table. "And make your own sandwich. I'm going for a bike ride."

Letting the backdoor slam behind her, Liz made a bee-line for the garage. In a few short motions, she was wearing her helmet and astride her faithful mountain bike. But as she wove around the housing development, Lizbeth discovered that the same leg pumping actions that purged her of the temper flare toward Amy were also causing unspeakable throbbing in her mound as her clit rubbed on the rounded leather saddle. *It's only fifty bucks, just give it to her now.*

THE NEXT EVENING, when Lizbeth opened the door for Beau Landry, she knew she'd lost the bet with Amy. With his broad shoulders accentuated by a light blue sports coat and a black V-neck T-shirt, she barely noticed the bouquet of baby's breath and pink orchestra mums he carried. His wavy blonde hair was pinned by a pair of black sunglasses, leaving those enticing cobalt eyes of his free to tease and tempt her.

"Hello, Lizbeth." His voice dropped an octave in greeting as he leaned forward to kiss her cheek. "These are for you." Placing the flowers in her arms, he stepped into the house when she nodded in silent invitation. His eyes seemed to widen with appreciation when they fell on the neckline of her seafoam green, linen dress. She felt her breasts flush with desire when Beau arched one eyebrow and smiled.

"Give me a moment." She looked down at the gift in her arms and turned toward the kitchen. Lizbeth's hands shook slightly when she retrieved a large clear glass vase from a side cabinet. Clutching it tightly, she moved to the sink and began filling it with water. *Stop shaking, you silly woman.*

Deep in concentration, analyzing her reaction, Liz didn't hear Beau enter the room. With a combination of surprise and titillation, she bumped the heavy container when his hand touched her cheek. She fumbled trying to avoid saturating her dress while righting the vase of delicate flowers in the sink, fighting the moan working its way to her lips.

"You look incredible." Beau's words caressed her earlobe from behind. Without warning, she felt his strong hands clasp her shoulders and turn her around, leaving his well-shaped lips just inches from hers. Unbidden, her own parted with desire and anticipation, her breath  hitching with need. Lizbeth felt the cold edge of the farmhouse sink against her bottom, giving her much needed support as the fire of Beau's kiss worked its magic over her. One hand slid around her waist while the other cradled her head. Wrapping her arms around his neck, she felt him step into her space with his broad chest and tapered waist greeting her intimately, as her hands left droplets of water on his sports coat.

Unlike their first kiss the night before, Beau was the one to break contact. Resting his forehead against hers while his chest heaved, his hands slid to the curve of her hips.

"We'll miss our reservation if we keep this up."

Liz giggled lightly. "I know. Plus," she paused for a second, breathing deeply, "you're wrinkling my dress and we haven't even gotten out the door."

"Well, we can't have either of us looking rumpled." He

cupped her face with both hands. "Even if we're both harboring tawdry thoughts."

He gave her a peck on the lips and turned to pick up the forgotten bouquet from the sink, sliding the flowers into the refilled vase. A few minutes later, they were heading north on Route 17, with Beau's hand resting comfortably in Lizbeth's lap.

## Chapter Five

As they drove to the restaurant, Liz grappled with her emotions. For as contradictory as it seemed, she could only describe her mood as calm excitement. There was no denying that everything about Beau turned her on and she loved that his large, muscular frame made her feel feminine, even though she was nearly as tall as him. From his strong hands to his tight ass in the black pants he wore, and the way his accent made every word feel like warm honey to her Northern ears, Lizbeth knew she was in dangerous territory. Add in the searing talent of his kisses, and she was pretty sure he should be classified as a lethal weapon.

But there was more to it than the obvious physical attributes. At some point since they left the winery, she'd made an unconscious decision to trust him. And it scared the crap out of her. *He's a perfect stranger.* She looked at his hand wrapped around her own, and then at his clean-shaven profile. Sensing her gaze as they pulled up to a traffic light, Beau turned to look at her. Rubbing his thumb over the tender pulse in her wrist, as his cobalt eyes sparked with desire, Liz felt her groin tighten with need. Everything

53

about him made Lizbeth wish she were in her twenties again. *Can I just throw caution to the wind? I want to, so badly.*

"Where are we going?" She forced the question out, intentionally breaking his spell before she succumbed and guided his hand under her dress.

"Alto Presco." With his free hand, he punctuated a faux Italian accent by kissing his finger tips and releasing it into the air. "One of a kind."

"Great. I prefer local restaurants to all those chains." She smiled in response. "Classic Italian fare?"

"Oh no." His deep laugh filled the car. "More like a fusion of beachy Asian seafood delights meets hibachi heat, with their own pasta made daily."

"Hhmm. Sounds unique."

Slipping his hand from her lap, Beau traced Liz's hairline, gently massaging the back of her neck. "Trust me."

*Oh my God, keep that up and I will.* Liz rolled her head into his hand.

"You'll like it."

When they entered the restaurant, Lizbeth was intrigued by her surroundings. As Beau had said, the surfside décor leaned formal with fully set tables anchored with crème colored linen. Even the delicate bamboo chairs were upholstered with the softly textured fabric. In several locations along the interior walls, there were tanks filled with brightly colored fish and the middle of the dining area was dominated by the sizzling excitement of several hibachi tables. Sitting diagonally to the water, two sides were open to a canopied deck, less than one hundred feet from the foaming water of the Atlantic Ocean. She couldn't resist smiling as they were led to an exterior table along the outside edge.

Browsing the menu in silence while they waited for their server to return with drinks, Lizbeth's vacillating mind leap-frogged from one delectable dish to the next. Despite the temptation of the meals that leaned Italian, she decided to try the restaurant's version of Tai.

When their drinks arrived, Beau leaned back in his chair, smiling at her. "Do you know what you'd like Lizbeth?"

Overcome by the urge to play with his double entendre, she placed her right hand on her décolletage, the tips of her long fingers lightly stroking the tanned softness of her own breast. With a slight nod, she arched one eyebrow and winked, enjoying Beau's reaction.

With their orders placed—yasai tempura and spicy bamboo with scallops for him and coconut soup with shrimp and drunken noodle for her—Liz searched for a polite topic of conversation. But each time she looked at the deep blue pools of Beau's eyes, she felt herself sway, knowing she'd go under if she didn't break contact.

And, when she did look away demurely, he seemed to take pleasure in it, his hearty chuckle causing her cheeks to flame. If only he knew what that laugh was doing to the rest of her body.

"Lizbeth, you don't have much to say for someone who teaches for a living." He leaned forward in his chair, allowing his arms to straddle the place setting in front of him, his fingertips drawing small circles on the creme linen. "Do I make you nervous?"

"No." She didn't dare look up, instead concentrating on the pattern his fingers created. "Just trying to figure out why, in a city with so many scantily clad young women, you wanted to have dinner with me."

She felt him lean across the intimate table, his fingers leaving the surface of it to gently cup her chin, the pads of his fingertips scorching her skin as he lifted it, so she was forced to look into his eyes.

"I've told you. I think you're beautiful. And, because you intrigue me."

Lizbeth struggled not to look away as he released her from the warmth of his hand. "Oh." She'd given him a chance to say something different, but he'd repeated his words from last night.

"In my book, an exceptional woman exudes the three Bs." His deep chuckle returned when she arched her right eyebrow in question. "Bright, bold, and beautiful." Lightly he outlined her lips with the tip of his index finger, pausing as a slight moan escaped from them. "Believe me, you have it all going on."

Her mind teetered on the edge of what felt like insanity while her body flushed with heat from the intimacy of his touch. Just as she was about to pull away from his grasp, the waiter returned with their appetizers. Trying to avoid conversation, Lizbeth happily began spooning the spicy coconut soup into her mouth, savoring the fiery sensation of galangal, lime and cilantro hitting the back of her tongue. When her bowl was empty, she removed her napkin from her lap and dabbed her mouth and then, finally, met Beau's gaze. And, he was smiling.

"Were you ravenous or did I embarrass you?"

"I— I was hungry. The salad I had for lunch left me hours ago." She pointed to his untouched food. "Those fried vegetables aren't going to taste all that great if you let them get cold."

She saw his eyes flicker down momentarily as he retrieved a string bean, dipped it in tempura sauce, and brought it to her lips. Parting them slightly, she allowed the salty and pungent moisture of soy sauce and dashi tease her mouth before she nipped off a piece of his offering and leaned back. "Now, you eat the rest."

Slowly, Beau unwrapped a set of the chopsticks left by

the waiter and worked his way through the side dish of vegetables. Liz admired how adept he was at using the wooden utensils, knowing her own fingers were helplessly uncoordinated despite the number of times she had tried to use them, causing her to resort to standard flatware to eat.

"You're good at using those. Do you eat a lot of Asian food?"

He treated her to another of his deep laughs as he answered her question. "Ha, ha. So, you think we're always eating things like hush puppies and corn dogs down here?"

Liz blushed profusely—this time from embarrassment, not lust. "No. I— I really hadn't given it much thought. But— but, yes. Maybe I did." Her stomach did a back flip as a smile split his face.

"That's all right, you're forgiven. We know that Northerners think we're bumpkins. But, South Carolina really is a lovely place. Maybe I can show you around a bit." He touched her forearm with his free hand, still cradling the chopsticks in the other. "We've the bucolic countryside of rolling hills, filled with sheep and cattle, and manor homes. Most people find the lanes of ancient oak trees draped in Spanish moss to be very romantic. And then, there's always Charleston for great music, bars, libraries, and museums."

She found herself grinning as she got caught up in his enthusiasm for his state. "I'll bet it's fabulous. But can I also get hush puppies and corn dogs?"

Laughing, Beau put down his chopsticks and grasped her hands. "You are delightful. Yes, you can have that to eat." His eyes locked her in their crystal embrace. "Please Lizbeth, say you'll let me show you around."

Taking a sip of the Riesling in her glass, her head spun

in a dizzying circle as she tried to absorb the insinuation of travelling with him. "But, I barely even know you."

"Believe me, I intend to change that." She watched as he drew her hands to his lips, the tip of his tongue searing the crevices between her fingers, her breath catching with each flick of sweetness. In her drought of intimacy, with the flames his look of lust conveyed to her, Liz tumbled down the rabbit hole, knowing she would owe Amy the fifty dollars before sunrise.

NEARLY TWO HOURS LATER, as they left the parking lot of Alto Presco, Beau turned to look at his date. "How about a walk on the beach to work off some of that meal?"

"A slow one, sure." She rested her hand on her belly. "I think I'm carrying about a ten-pound food baby here." Liz's self-deprecating laugh made him smile.

"How do you feel about parking at my house?" He saw her swallow before answering.

"Um, sure. That makes sense, I guess."

Beau felt an awkward silence fill the car as she looked out the side window. *Fortunately, it's a quick trip. Don't blow this Landry.*

A few minutes later, he pulled into the circular drive-way, put the SUV into park, and quickly moved around the front of the car to open Lizbeth's door. With her hand gently cradled in his, Beau led her up the sweeping marble staircase to the front door, where he keyed in a few numbers, activating an auto-butler. Soundlessly, the solid wood swung inward, as soft lights switched on, bathing the inside of the house in a warm embrace.

Beau pulled Lizbeth into his arms, teasing her soft lips with a brief kiss. "Welcome to my home."

As they stepped inside, he saw Liz's eyes sweep the open floor plan. With a smile plastered on her delicate face, she pointed to the bank of windows on the far side of the kitchen. "Wow." She crossed the room to stand facing the water. "What a view."

"Thank you." Even though she had been on the back porch, she had not been inside, and he was pleased she admired the house—one he had designed and contracted himself. Beau joined her by the wall of glass to enter another security code. Within seconds, the series of thermal pane panels began moving, allowing the salt air and the music of the crashing waves to ride in on the sundown breeze.

After draping his sports coat over a dining room chair and slipping off his loafers, Beau extended his hand to Lizbeth. "Shall we? The beach awaits us."

Leaning lightly on his hand, he watched her step out of her sandals. Her head tipped coquettishly as she giggled, her voice dropping into a sweet drawl. "Why, sir. I believe we shall."

Beau held her hand as they crossed the back porch. At the bottom step, he lifted Lizbeth's left one a moment, signaling her to stand still while he stepped into the sand. Under her curious watch, he propped his right foot on the wood and cuffed his pants to mid-calf, then did the same with the other leg. Next, without a word, he placed his hands on her waist and lifted her.

"Oh," Beau heard Liz utter in surprise as she steadied herself on his shoulders. Slowly, he slid her lissome body down the front of his, savoring the pressure of her breasts against his own chest. Encouraging her to step into his embrace, Beau felt her slight tremble as his hand slipped up her back to rest on the nape of her neck. His lips met the luscious curves of her mouth. He traced their surface with his tongue until they parted for him.

"Oohh." The sweet, single syllable glided from her mouth to his, sending a surge of need directly to his groin. Beau struggled not to slide his hands under her dress to hold her firmly against his erection, to cup her incredibly taut derriere, to move deeper to stroke her womanhood.

*Oh, Christ. I'd like to have her right here on the steps.* He leaned back from the kiss as that thought entered his mind. "Ready for our walk?"

"If you can promise we'll get back to that kiss when we return to the house." Lizbeth licked her lips.

"I think it can be arranged." His voice, husky with desire, as she leaned back into his chest a moment before responding.

"I like a man who keeps his word." He saw her wink just as she took off toward the water. Beau enjoyed the view for a minute, then joined Lizbeth in the surf, playfully splashing her golden legs with his own exaggerated jumping steps. Her laughter tugged at his heart strings.

"Hey, you." He tucked her left hand in his, drawing her close. Nuzzling her neck, Beau lost himself in the heady sensation of her perfume, the slap of water on his feet and the slight moan she emitted as she slid her arms around his middle.

"Do we have to walk?"

Beau leaned back in surprise to look at her eyes. "Do you have a different idea?"

"Yes." She took in a deep breath. "For now, how 'bout we just stand here, pretending that the sand isn't moving with each wave."

He kissed her lightly. "And, for later?"

Beau watched her head dip as a light blush filled her cheeks.

"Um. I— I was thinking…"

He placed his index finger under her chin, so she would look up at him. "As the saying goes, I'm all ears."

Lizbeth shifted in the waning sand, raising her foot so her strong thigh pressed against his package. "Seems to me you're more than just ears." She moistened her lips and grinned.

He admired the mischievous sparkle in her eyes as a deep, rumbling laugh filled his chest. "What I am is a healthy, heterosexual male holding an incredibly sexy woman in my arms while standing in the warm surf of the Atlantic Ocean at sunset. This is a turn-on."

While he loved looking at her eyes, her lips were simply too tempting. Ignoring the other evening beach-goers, Beau claimed Lizbeth in another deep, tantalizing dance. This time he only pulled away when he felt himself go off balance on the unstable shore.

"So." His thumb teased the tender skin below her earlobe. "You had another idea?"

"Ah, yes." Liz moved her hand across his pecs, stopping momentarily to tease each nipple, down his taut abs and stopped at his belt. Beau felt his breath hitch as she inserted her fingers into his waistband and gave a slight tug. "But we'll be arrested if we do it here." Her free hand made a wide sweeping gesture indicating the beach. Without another word, she tugged on his belt and lead him back to the house while he silently thanked his housekeeper for taking a week off, leaving them total privacy.

CROSSING the sand to Beau's house, Liz wouldn't let herself think about what she was doing. In all the years of her marriage bed, she had never been the one to initiate their intimacy. Fearful her late husband would think she was cheap, or worse yet, accuse her of being a whore, Lizbeth never made demands. Nor did she ever comment when their love making was less than satisfactory for her—which was frequently.

Flirting with Beau, being forward and familiar with his body—none of it had been easy for her. But, somehow, being nearly one thousand miles from her normal life, she felt free from the shackles of propriety. Yeah, she knew it sounded like a cliché, but she didn't care. Instead, she would embrace Amy's advice, with every intention of leading this very virile man into his house to act out all those delectable scenes she'd read in countless romance novels. *Maybe I'll even ride him like a cowgirl!* But, as they climbed the porch steps, she paused when her confidence slipped a notch. *I've only had one man in my life. What if I suck at this? Maybe I should tell him.* She felt Beau's arm slip around her shoulder.

"Are you sure about this?" His sweet baritone soothed her nerves. "Ya know, we can wait. Get to know each other better."

She tried not to swoon over his gesture, especially since she knew he had a throbbing erection going on. Lizbeth looked into his crystal blue eyes for a moment, knowing what she'd been missing for years. "I've never been more sure." She leaned in to kiss him and then dragged him in through the wall of glass.

As soon as the panels latched securely into place, Beau pulled her to him, his hands cupping her derriere, firmly holding her hips against his bulging erection. He swayed slightly so that his shirt played back and forth with her breasts, each pass across her hardening points sent her body spiraling, weakening her knees, causing her to lean into him for support.

"Beau, there's something I need to tell you." A surging shiver of excitement coursed through her abdomen when he leaned back, and she saw the smoldering, hooded lust in his eyes. Without responding, his head dipped. He planted kisses on her neck, each one igniting a new burst of fire in her groin. Through the delicate fabric of her linen dress, he cupped her left breast, his thumb caressing her nipple. Liz's reaction was almost painful as he continued to toy with the already sensitive tips trapped within her bra. Each stroke of his hand fanned the embers below.

Breathless with aching need, Lizbeth was startled when Beau's lips ceased their magic. She opened her eyes to see him pointing across the living room to a broad, sweeping stair case.

"You're still sure?"

She nodded.

"The bedroom is on the third floor. Care to join me?"

All she could do was grin.

Beau took her hand. At the bottom of the polished oak, he waved his hand over a small, glass disc, turning off the lights on the first floor while triggering a warm, luminous path to the next floor. When they reached the top, there was a single door, which opened as they approached.

"Wait here a second. Please."

Lizbeth stood just inside the doorway, awestruck by the classy opulence of the space. She watched as Beau waved his hand over yet another motion sensitive switch on the far wall. While the large window slid open, the muscles in his runner's butt flexed invitingly when he turned back to face her and pointed to a large credenza on one wall.

"I'd offer you music, but I prefer the song of the surf."

Another grin was her only response when he motioned her toward him. *Holy crap. Not only is his body beyond hot, but his personality is cute!* Lizbeth reached for his head, steering his lips to hers. She ached to plunder his mouth to relieve some of the heat and pressure building in her pelvis. But after a few kisses, he pulled away from her.

"No, darlin'." He looked down at her. "I'm leading this party." A teasing smile played on his handsome face as he slid his hand down her hips and under her dress, inching his way inside, his fingers slipping under the lace waistband of her panties. His large hand causing shots of fire throughout her body.

She tried moving as his fingers dipped lower, but there was no escaping his firm hold. Trapped but excited, her inner thighs ached with anticipation, just waiting for him to stroke her nub. A small whimper escaped her lips. *How much longer?* She wanted him to give her more.

He started kissing her neck, again. Her earlobes, again. Torture on both ends. And then his tongue was in her mouth. Darting in and out. Teasing, touching, plunging. In and out. In and out. She was so caught up in the fever pitch in her mouth, she didn't realize that Beau had undone her dress, until it slid off her shoulders, exposing her nipples as they strained against her lace bra. Seconds later, his large hand slid inside her panties and his middle finger began to dance on her clit, keeping the same tempo as his tongue. Flicking up and down, the fire raged. His tongue darting, his finger flicking. Then, he plunged. Multiple fingers, sliding in and out, with each trip going deeper and harder until she exploded, growling as her body convulsed with her release. Liz let go, collapsing in the strength of his arms and slid into the oblivion of her orgasm.

She felt Beau gently massaging her temples, bringing her back to the present. Laying on his bed, it felt like a dream. She looked into his eyes. "How did I get here? Did I fall asleep?"

"Mmmm, sort of." The corner of his mouth twitched with the start of a grin. "You definitely passed out." His hand moved from her temple to cup her breast. "But judging by the sounds you were making, I'd say it was more like you fell off a cliff, not asleep."

Shifting her gaze out a nearby window, Lizbeth felt a warm blush fill her cheeks as self-doubt swamped her head. *What just happened? I acted like an animal. And the lights were on!*

She felt the bed shift as Beau stood up. Turning her head, she found him undressing. Slowly, agonizingly so, he opened the buttons on his shirt, each one revealing more of his chiseled chest and taut abs. He dropped it to the floor, then unbuckled his belt and peeled off his still-cuffed pants, leaving a lightweight pair of briefs holding his immense bulge.

She closed her eyes for just a moment with a virgin's blush heating her face—her late husband had never stripped in front of her. When she opened them, Beau slid his shorts down off his hips, his erect manhood proudly pointing at her. Liz smiled, openly admiring the raw beauty of the intimate moment.

Extending a hand to her, Beau pulled her to stand next to him while he began removing her undergarments. Any common sense Liz still possessed after the orgasm was quickly extinguished when he scooped up her naked body and laid her back on the sheets. His hands immediately began travelling down her abdomen, leaving a searing path from her breasts to her mound, igniting goose bumps on her flesh where her clothing had been.

Dropping to one knee by the bed, he guided her right hand to her vagina, encouraging Lizbeth to stroke herself while he watched. After a few minutes, he pulled her hand to his mouth laving her fingers with his tongue, sucking her juice from them while his other hand slipped between her thighs. Liz's hips bucked, trying to force his fingers deeper inside to relieve the aching. As her shudders  returned, Beau pulled out his fingers, standing quickly, pulling her up to him, spinning her around, his erection pressing into the small of her back.

She felt her ears tingle with heat as he delivered a teasing whisper. "Not yet, gorgeous." The tip of his tongue started tracing the delicate folds. "It's too soon for you to come." She gasped as he buried his tongue deep in her ear while his fingers found her nub. Just as her legs were about to give out, he withdrew again, spinning her around to face him. His lips met hers, his tongue probing and pillaging, sucking her whimpering breath into his own mouth before drawing away.

He lifted her hands over her head, pulling her close to him, causing her nipples to graze his hairy chest. She swayed slightly, the texture causing more heat in her groin. Overcome with hunger, she began nibbling on the base of his neck. She kissed the hollow and then ran her tongue up to the slight lump of his Adam's apple. Standing on her toes, she was able to reach his earlobes, quickly sucking one into her mouth before  he put  his hand on her shoulders, preventing her from kissing him further.

Beau's fingers cupped her buttocks, delving deeper and teasing her aching vulva from behind. She struggled to think coherently. He lowered his head, his tongue tickled and teased her mouth, her legs began to spread, allowing three of his fingers to glide back and forth, the pressure increasing with each pass.

Without warning, Lizbeth felt herself swaying without his support. Her eyes flew open in shock, only to find him returning to her side with a small white package. The blue of his eyes swirling darker with lust as he extracted the condom and handed it to her. "Would you?"

Delicately, she held the latex disc in her lips and ran her hands down the side of his hips as she sunk to her knees in front of him. Resisting the urge to giggle as the straining head of his penis bumped her face, Liz transferred the condom to her right hand while she touched his balls with her left. Beau moaned as she gently massaged his sack with her thumb and forefinger. Encouraged by his reaction, Lizbeth cast aside all her germ-a-phobe tendencies and shifted her head, so she was able to run her tongue along the underside of his quivering shaft.

"Oh, yeah." Beau's fingers sank into her hair.

Liz rolled the latex protection over his member while it was moist from her teasing. Then she slipped his engorged head past her lips, causing Beau to buck, sending his shaft deep into her mouth for a few manic thrusts of his hips.

Then, pulling his pelvis back from her head, he lifted Liz to stand in front of him, his forehead leaning against hers as he spoke. "It will be the end if you keep that up." Cupping her face, he kissed her lips. "And I want to make love to you. To be inside you when I come."

The southern honey of his promise fanned her own need. She arched her hips, silently asking for more, but he waited another minute before simultaneously plunging his tongue in her mouth while his fingers invaded her molten core. Just as she was about to explode, Beau quickly lowered her to the bed, positioning himself between her legs. He lifted her bottom, wrapping her legs around his waist. His tongue tortured her mouth, trapping her scream of ecstasy when his helmet pressed against her throbbing clit with each pass of his penis, driving deeper inside of her with each stroke, again and again, finally growling with his own release.

Fifteen minutes later, when he led her to take a shower with him, his free hand lifted her chin, meeting her eyes. "You are magnificent."

A giggle escaped her lips as he pulled her into the cool tiled floor of the walk-in shower and turned on the faucet. Cascading hot water from the rain-forest style head wrapped Liz as Beau lathered, foamed, and massaged every inch of her body. He suckled her breasts until they peaked into painful burning points, the whole time teasing her nub with a random finger. Then, leaning her against the back wall, he manipulated her with the hand-held showerhead until she convulsed with her release, falling into his arms.

## Chapter Six

*Lizbeth awoke* to the annoying ding of an incoming text message on her cell phone. Rolling over and defensively blocking her eyes from the morning daylight, she struggled for a moment to identify the massive bed where she was lying. Grabbing the pillow next to her, she drew in a long breath, immediately sending herself back to the magic of the previous night with Beau. *Oh yes, that's where I am. But where is my phone?*

Looking across the room, she saw the green linen garment in a pile with Beau's black slacks and shirt. "Flip." She grumbled at the unappealing idea of leaving the luxurious sheets and comforter to fetch her phone, but serious guilt over not letting Amy and Carolee know where she was won out.

When her bare feet had to leave the plush rug for hardwood, Liz scowled at the air conditioner blasting cold across the floor. Grabbing her dress, she jumped back to the rug, leaning on the pillow-topped mattress while fishing her slim phone from the nearly invisible side pocket. She tapped on the icon bearing Amy's name.

Are you okay?

Her fingers moved across the key pad. Yes. All is good.

Did you have hot sex with him?

Liz stood shaking her head at her friend's boldness. Go to work. I'm fine.

Not wanting to engage in back and forth texts regarding her intimacy with Beau, Lizbeth silenced her phone, slid it back into the pocket and draped her dress over a leather Queen Anne chair. Looking around the room, she realized there was a folded piece of paper on the bedside table with her name on it.

L – went for a run. Make yourself at home. You'll find coffee in the walk-in closet/nook. B

She liked the blocky script of his hand writing. And, since he invited her to do so, she moved into what she would have called a small bedroom, not a closet. She found several suits and casual outfits, along with polished bamboo built-in drawers and shelves holding shoes and extra bedding. There was a panel hiding an ironing board and a small barista station. But before she made coffee, she needed to find something to wear. Lizbeth ran her hand along the hanging shirts until she came across a cream-colored light weight cotton shirt. With the top three buttons undone, she slipped it over her head, pleased to have it fall to her upper thigh.

Feeling less exposed, she turned to several stainless-steel appliances. Unsure of what each did, she slipped one of the stacked coffee mugs under the spout of the single serve machine, popped a disposable pod into the top basket and closed the lid. Pressing the flashing blue button, she stood for a moment while the intoxicating scent of dark coffee filled the room. When she was sure the pot was done dripping, she left to find a comfortable seat. Waving her hand over the same motion sensitive disc that Beau had used the night before, she opened the door facing the beach.

Stepping out of the air-conditioned house, the southern morning wrapped itself around Lizbeth like a hot towel, the salty moisture seeping into the skin of her sleepy body. Palming her coffee cup, she stood on the deck watching the waves undulating on the shore, their ceaseless crashing mesmerizing her.

As she settled into a generous teak chair, Liz watched the beach wake up under the relentless South Carolina heat. People walked in pairs, some with dogs, others just side-by-side in familiar step. One man took several swings of his arm, finally casting the end of his fishing rod fifty feet from the shore, the silvery line glittering as it flew through the air.

A small pickup truck drove down beach to a large wooden container where two younger men got out. After a few loud shouts, they opened the front of the box and extracted equipment. She watched as one of them set out lounge chairs and the other made tapping noises on white pipes in the sand. Minutes later, he slid an umbrella into each holder, popping them open in the morning breeze.

Looking across the water, Lizbeth realized that two boats bobbed in the surf, about two hundred yards out. She'd seen their beacon the night before, constantly flickering as the boats were tossed in the rough water. A single *Sea-doo* towing what looked like a giant banana approached the first boat. Liz squinted, willing her aging eyes to focus on the activity, but the people on the craft looked like ants and they disappeared in each trough of the ocean.

Suddenly, a giant splay of color popped up from the first boat. Red, blue and yellow striped fabric danced behind the vessel in the wind-tossed sky. As the craft started to move, it took mere seconds for the parachute to travel about a hundred feet skyward. Dangling human legs were barely discernable as the boat slowly moved south in the water.

Lizbeth watched the boat make several passes before reeling the parachute back in, dropping the people into it. As if on cue, the *Sea-doo* crossed over from the other vessel. Straining to catch the action, she lifted her cooling coffee to her lips, accidentally spilling some on the tails of Beau's shirt. "Oh, crap." Liz tried to wipe the moisture off as quickly as she could. When she heard the engine of the *Sea-doo* come back to life, she forgot about the possible stain and watched the pilot of the water craft playfully towing the banana boat back to shore, weaving back and forth across the waves, somehow managing to avoid the deep troughs. With his passengers safely on shore, she marveled as the machine raced over the open water again, the driver standing to absorb the powerful slapping of the waves.

Looking east as the sun slipped behind some clouds, Lizbeth appreciated the momentary overcast conditions. On the far horizon, the slate blue water turned into a faint green and then brown, in the churning and roiling surf. Had there been sunshine, it would have glared off the surface and diminished the deep color of the ocean. With her curiosity about the parachutes settled, she made herself more coffee and returned to check out the burgeoning action on the sand just as the sun pushed its way through the clouds.

*Where is he?* It dawned on Liz that she'd been up for over half an hour and Beau had yet to return from his run. Her eyes scanned the Atlantic sand from her third-floor perch off the master bedroom, locking in on a jogging male figure. As he came closer, she saw his pumping arms cause massive pecs to flex and rock with each movement. The sun highlighted the gold flecks in his wind-blown hair as he splashed through the shallow depths of the water. When he was parallel to the house, Beau turned to face her. With his back to the brilliant gold of the sun, his handsome face was lost in the silhouette. But Lizbeth knew he was smiling by the tone of his voice as he shouted in greeting and waved.

"'Mornin'. I'll be right up." His sexy voice reached her as he left the hard-packed sand to reach the porch on the first floor.

Liz contemplated going down to greet him, but sipping her coffee won out. A minute later, she heard the glass panel behind her slide open, bringing a blast of cool air and a very sexy, sweaty, and virile Beau Landry with it.

"Good morning, gorgeous." Lizbeth's nipples stood at attention under her borrowed shirt when he kissed her neck, then her ear, then her lips, all while she cradled the mug of coffee. Beau's hand slipped down from her shoulders, his thumbs lightly grazing the sensitive peaks and cupping her breasts. "Nice shirt."

"You seemed to have a few spares." She winked at him in response. "And I didn't feel like putting on my dress." Liz watched the solid muscles in his well-toned thighs flex as he sat in the chair next to her.

Placing a full bottle of water on the small table that separated them, Beau reached out for her hand. Raising it to his lips, he planted a moist kiss on the back and then he nibbled on the edges of each finger, his darting tongue teasing the sensitive and soft skin between them.

Liz took a swallow of coffee to hide the reaction of her traitorous body, willing her breath to steady. She fought against the need to shift in her seat as heat filled her throbbing pussy. *Good lord, you're making the chair wet.*

"I'm glad you didn't put on your dress."

Meeting the hooded gaze in Beau's eyes, Liz gave in

and licked her lips, sucking the lower one in with an almost imperceptible moan.

"You saved me the trouble of ripping it off of you." In a single, swift, motion, he stood, pulling her up to his still drying chest. "I don't care what happens to this shirt." He slipped his hands under the crisp tails. Massaging the rounds of her buttocks, he kept her snug to his pecs and snuck a few fingers in to tease her from behind. "Ready for breakfast?"

"Uumm, yes." Lizbeth wasn't sure if he meant food or sex, but either way she was ravenous. She set the empty coffee cup on the table and followed Beau's extended hand into the bedroom.

When he led her directly to the bed instead of downstairs to the kitchen, she sighed in anticipation of a repeat of the blush-worthy things he'd done to her the night before. With just inches between them, Liz saw the solid hard-on pressing against the light fabric of Beau's running shorts. Torn between holding his member or kissing him, she opted to pay attention to his impressive chest. With her hands on his hips, Lizbeth ran her tongue in lazy circles around his defined muscles. She saw his package flexing with need as she licked the slightly salty skin. A deep groan rumbled from within when she flicked across his hard nipples, then grazed them with the edge of her teeth.

Beau lifted her head, his mouth crushing hers. Deep and rapid, she took his frenetic kiss, wrapping her mouth around his probing tongue, sliding back and forth, sucking him until his breath came in ragged gasps. In a sudden single rend, his big hands grabbed the shirt she was wearing just above her décolletage, the sound of popping buttons sending bolts of heat to Liz's already throbbing mound.

"Animal." She threw her head back with wickedly,

theatrical laughter as Beau crushed her hips to his. Wrapping her leg around him, she ground her heat against his bare thigh, knowing he could feel her moisture.

Spinning them around, Beau held one hand as he gently pushed her to the bed. "I know." He slid her legs apart, racing his fingers up her inner thigh, dipping between her aching lips. "And now I'm going to eat you for breakfast."

When he dropped to his knees next to the bed, burying his face in her tender flesh, Lizbeth cupped her ample breasts in her own hands, stroking her nipples while Beau's fingers and tongue pillaged her pussy. Half delight, half torture, he kept it up until she was powerless to control the bucking of her hips, driving him into her as deeply as she could, crashing with sweet release.

AFTER HIS SHOWER, Beau found Lizbeth sitting on the deck off his bedroom, the late morning sun catching on the light, tawny skin of her upper thighs. This time she had on one of his V-neck white Ts. *She's incredible.* He watched for a moment as she raised a bottle of water to her lips, the condensation sliding down to drip on the apex of her bosom as she emptied the container. Giggling, she slid her hand between her voluptuous and unfettered breasts, causing a rush of heat to fill his groin. *Holy crap old man. You better pick up more condoms.*

Beau hoped the past sixteen hours hadn't just been a fluke. He truly enjoyed spending time with Lizbeth. Not only was she bright, funny, and athletic, but—unlike many of the women he'd had in his bed in recent years —she was close to his age. There was a distinct sexiness in the way she told him what she wanted in bed. And what she wanted, had been more daring than he'd expected.

But, there was more to it than just the hot sex. At the risk of sounding like a sap, he hoped that Liz was enjoying his company, in addition to his manhood. Because, he was certainly smitten with her.

Grabbing a bottle of water from the small fridge in the nook, Beau moved out to the deck and stood behind Lizbeth's chair. With his hands on her shoulders, she leaned into his touch, tilted her face to the sky and smiled as she accepted the cold drink. "What are you watching doll?"

She pointed to the horizon with her long, slender fingers. "The parasailing. It intrigues me."

"Ever been?" Beau found himself gently massaging her neck.

"No. But it looks like fun."

Beau leaned down and kissed the side of her cheek. "Then, let's go. Get dressed."

Liz spun around in her chair with an unreadable look on her face. Fear, excitement, curiosity? He wasn't sure.

"Well? Do you want to try it?" He held one hand up in question as the other pointed toward the water.

In seconds she was standing in front of him, holding the bottom edge of the t-shirt she wore. "But I only have a dress to wear."

"So, put it on and we'll swing by your house for more suitable clothing." The words were barely out of his mouth before she sprinted in to change while her laughter floated out to the deck. He waited a moment and then joined her at the door of his bedroom.

"All set." Lizbeth's smile reminded him of a small child at Christmas. Her bare feet made soft tapping noises as she raced down the oak staircase and to the back door of the house to grab her sandals. Within minutes they were in his SUV, making short work of the trip across Route 17 to her house.

When they pulled up to the modest ranch, Liz leaned across the console and kissed him. "Mmmm. I'll be right back."

"You got it." As soon as she was inside, Beau used his phone to call his friends at Top Sail. A few years back, when he'd been building his house on the beach, Beau had invested in the start up company because he liked the work ethic of Tyler, the late twenty-something owner. The youngest child in the family that owned the Parasail Winery, Tyler wanted to try something "off the farm." Having spent most of his lifetime under the strong hand of his own father, Beau appreciated the willpower it took to walk away from the security of a family business. He made a five-year investment deal into Top Sail, allowing Tyler enough cash flow to establish himself in Myrtle Beach and Hilton Head Island for the summer months. And in Miami Beach and Key West for the winter months. With his money long since doubled and repaid, Beau took every opportunity he could to visit with Tyler and throw him some business.

Finishing his phone call just as Lizbeth came out of the house, his eyes were glued to her. He was a little let down to see that she'd encumbered her magnificent breasts in a sports bra, preventing them from moving easily under the tank top she had on. *Naked. They should be naked and free!* Now that he had had the privilege of seeing her completely undressed, even though he knew it seemed ridiculous, he wanted her to stay naked. He shook his head a moment when he realized that he was thinking like the domineering old men of his father's generation. *You're not that kind of asshole, Landry.*

"What's the matter?" Liz's brows were furrowed. "Are you pouting?"

"No. Not exactly." He waited for her to buckle her seat belt before putting the Mercedes in gear. "Honestly?"

Lizbeth placed her hand on his arm before answering. "Yes. Always honestly."

"I prefer you naked."

Beau pulled to the side of the street when her barking laughter filled the car. "Oh, my God." She pressed her hand to chest, causing her breasts to jiggle, adding to Beau's consternation. "When I said, 'always honestly,' I meant don't lie to me." She continued to laugh as he unhooked his seat belt and leaned across the console and kissed her, until both were short on breath.

"I can't help it. You have a magnificent body. And now I've seen every inch of it." He watched the flush cover her cheeks. "As a matter of fact, now that I've teased, licked and kissed every inch of it, I know I prefer to see you naked."

"You're pretty good-looking in your birthday suit, yourself." She braced herself on his right arm while leaning across him to affectionately cup his expanding junk. "And if we keep this up, I'll never get to go parasailing."

"Alright, alright." He kissed her hand and re-buckled his seat belt before moving the car again. "After we're done, let's find something to eat." When she responded with a coquettish giggle, he figured she was thinking of sex. "I really meant food this time."

AS BEAU PULLED into the beachside parking lot, Lizbeth had to admit she was nervous. Very excited, but a little nervous. *What if there are sharks? What if the ropes break? What if you fall out of the harness and drop one hundred feet to your death?*

Swallowing, she pulled out her phone to distract herself by sending a text to Amy.

Going parasailing.

**You crazy brat. Wait for me**. Liz smiled at her friend's response.

Going with Beau

The sex must have been incredible!!!! This time she laughed out loud.

Get back to work. I'll see you for dinner.

Beau left the SUV for a moment and then opened her door. "You planning on taking that thing with you?" He pointed to her cell phone.

Liz dropped it into the pocket on her door. "Nope." Standing up, she pressed her body to his—to feel his solid pecs, but also to gain some support before she could chicken out. Wrapping her arm around his waist, she smiled up at him and summoned her inner cheerleader. "Let's go!"

# Chapter Seven

Liz stood between a rack of life vests and a pop-up tent watching Beau in animated conversation with a heavily muscled man in his mid-thirties, wishing they could get moving. As if reading her mind, Beau turned to her, crossed the open space in a few steps, with the stranger by his side.

"Lizbeth, this is Tyler. He's the owner."

She extended her right hand to receive the younger man's offered shake.

"He's going to take us out and captain the boat we'll be using."

Liz nodded politely, afraid that her voice would crack with nervousness if she spoke, burying her hands as far into her pockets as the fabric would allow. If Beau delayed this experience any longer, she was going to faint from anxiety.

"Grab a vest." Tyler inclined his head to the rack behind her.

When she pulled a large from the rack, the owner

shook his head and suggested a medium. "You want it snug."

Lizbeth took a hot pink one, while Beau's was in caution yellow. Once his own vest was secure, he stood in front of Liz, blocking her view of the ocean. With his hands pulling the end of the black strap surrounding her waist, he leaned into her ear, whispering softly. "Relax, baby. You're going to love this."

*Relax? I'm about to toss my cookies. And this thing is so freaking tight I can barely breathe.* Seemingly oblivious to her increasing fear, Beau took her hand and led her into the surf to mount the waiting banana-shaped raft. He watched while she straddled the rough canvas and tightly grasped the rubber handle, and then settled himself in the next position. Tyler sat in the middle on the opposite pontoon to balance out their weight.

Without warning, the operator of the *Sea-doo* gunned the engine, causing the water craft to spin quickly. In seconds, the tow rope connecting the two snapped taut and the banana boat took off with a jolt, leaving Liz hanging on in desperation. As they broke through the first set of waves, she squeezed her knees to the canvas as tightly as she could, but her ass still became airborne. An unrecognizable scream flew from her mouth when the raft crashed down in the next wave, her weight slamming her spine causing instant agony while splashing salt water covered her face, nearly blinding her. As the craft pulled them over the next wall of water, Lizbeth heard Beau shouting encouragement for her to 'hang in there.'

After what might have been the longest two minutes of her life, the *Sea-doo* slowed to a crawl for the banana boat to come parallel to a mid-size vessel. Two men on the boat waved in greeting to Tyler; one of them offered Liz a much-needed hand so she was able to step from the raft to the deck of the larger boat. Once all three of them were on board, the water craft made short work of returning to the shore, where Lizbeth assumed another group of uninformed customers were about to get their own two minutes of torture.

"Hey, beautiful." Beau slipped an arm around her waist, steering her toward the back of the boat. "We're going to put on these harnesses and sit on this deck, in front of the parachute."

Liz tried to suppress her skepticism when she looked down at the small amount of metal and plywood he referred to as a deck. *It'll be some major miracle if I get out of this alive!*

"Don't worry, it'll hold both of us."

He handed the first harness to her, but her arms refused to move to slide into it.

Beau placed his hands on her shoulders. "We don't have to do this if you've changed your mind."

Too stubborn to admit to her fear, Lizbeth shook her head and grabbed the heavy neoprene straps from him.

With both harnesses secured, the boat bobbed in the ocean as she and Beau sat on the deck.

First, Tyler connected the parachute to rings at their waistlines. Then, he clipped a giant pile of coiled rope to a strap that ran between them.

"We'll start out slow. But Lizbeth," Tyler looked her in the eye. "I've gotta move quick after that or you'll sink and be trapped in the water with that parachute. Okay?"

She nodded mutely, hoping none of the men could see how frightened she was, or that her traitorous stomach wanted to embarrass her with each pitch of the boat.

*Lord, please do not make today my day to die. Amen.*

Liz had to admit that she had never been terribly religious, something she was seriously regretting right now.

She hoped that any higher power that was listening would not be holding a grudge over her lack of participation in church activities.

Looking down at her feet as she contemplated her fate, Lizbeth didn't see Tyler move to the front of the boat and her head jerked up just as it started to move. *Not ready yet!* Her thought didn't get a chance to reach her lips before the throttle increased, propelling the boat forward.

"Holy shit!" She heard herself scream when the parachute filled with air, launching them up behind the shrinking vessel. Her grip on the harness was so severe that her hands ached as she watched the rope binding her to safety continue to uncoil.

And then, she realized they were fully airborne, and she was still alive. Relief flooded her as she turned to look at Beau, who was grinning like the proverbial Cheshire cat.

Lizbeth looked around. To her left, the buildings on the shore seemed like toys and people were mere specks. To her right, the ocean went on forever. Big, blue, and glistening, with the occasional white cap breaking the surface. It felt incredible, like she was weightless, floating through the sky. And it was quiet. So very quiet that she could hear Tyler talking to his employees.

"What do ya think, darlin'?" Beau's drawl sounded sexier than usual.

"This is so incredible." She hoped Beau understood the sense of joy racing through her. Liz felt like every fiber in her body was charged. Like she was experiencing a never-ending orgasm.

They traveled north for a little while, each of them pointing out familiar buildings along the beach. Then the boat turned away from the shore in a large arcing sweep.

After fifteen minutes of floating over the water, she heard the engine slow and realized that she and Beau were being pulled down to the boat. A few yards before they reached the deck, their feet dangled in the tepid waves momentarily as the parachute lost air. The three men reeled them in, gently setting their feet on the deck. She felt Beau steady her as they moved into the back of the boat.

Wearing a goofy grin, Lizbeth leaned against his solid frame while she found her sea legs in the pitching boat. Before she knew it, the deck hands from Top Sail were guiding her back to the banana boat and the *Sea-doo* was returning them to shore.

"I CANNOT BELIEVE I just did that!" Lizbeth shouted excitedly at Beau as they raced across the hot sand to reach his car. With her hands stretched above her head, she spun in circles. "It was awesome."

Grabbing him by the hand, she pulled Beau to her body, crushing her breasts against his chest as she hugged him. "Thank you so much. You taught me to fly. How can I ever repay you?" She gave him a quick kiss and then spun in a few more circles until he guided her to his Mercedes.

Once inside the much-needed air conditioning, he picked up her hand, giving her one of his signature nuzzlings. "Darlin', you are most welcome." He waited a moment. "Your excitement is payment enough." Leaning across the console, he pulled Lizbeth into his arms, cradling the back of her head with his well-defined bicep. "Let's get some lunch, okay?" But, before she could answer, his mouth covered hers, his tongue teasing her lips with reminders of the past eighteen hours. Then, as he leaned back from her and settled into the driver's seat, she nodded in response, smiling broadly as Beau drove them away from the parking lot.

An hour later, fully sated by a cobb salad and what seemed like a gallon of iced sweet tea, they left the diner for the grocery store. As they pulled up to the *Piggly Wiggly*, Liz started laughing when she realized it was the same one where Carolee's man-friend worked, and where she and Beau first met.

Crossing the parking lot, he wrapped his arm around her shoulder. "You remember?"

"Ha." She bumped his hip affectionately. "How could I not?"

Just inside the door, she motioned to a line of silver carts. "Do we need one?"

"Nah. You said you've got lots of fresh produce. We'll just get stuff like the shrimp, Andouille sausage, and crab-meat. And, my favorite Cajun seasoning." He leaned down and grabbed a hard, plastic basket from a rack. "You northerners have never had good gumbo until you've had Beau Landry's delightful creation."

That honeyed baritone made her groin surge at the word delightful. But, Liz didn't want to burst his bubble by telling him she had never had gumbo and doubted that Amy or Carolee had either since it wasn't a staple on most Albany menus. When eating lunch, he got all excited telling her about his cooking prowess. Then his teenage boy-like exuberance rolled into suggesting he make dinner for all of them. And even though she expected some serious chop busting from the younger women, Lizbeth was looking forward to spending the evening with them all together.

※※

WHILE LIZBETH TOOK A SHOWER, Beau moved about the kitchen of the rental she shared with her friends, familiarizing himself with the utensils and food stores that were available. Pulling sweet Vidalias, bell peppers, celery, parsley, and green onions from the bottom compartment of the fridge, he dropped all of it into the sink. As he peeled, rinsed, and diced the produce, he thought about his day spent with Liz.

The first thing to pop into his head was the mind-blowing sex. And while her hunger seemed insatiable, she gave equally to what she received. He loved it when a woman was bold and assertive in bed. It just so happened that this particular beauty had killer long legs and sumptuous breasts that added to the package. With the thought of her warm flesh pressed against him, somewhere between cutting the celery and peeling raw shrimp, the soft sound of Liz singing in the shower had triggered his memory of the near guttural expressions she made each time she climaxed.

*Shit!* Beau nearly stabbed his palm with the paring knife when unexpected hands cupped his ass. He'd been so wrapped up in naked vignettes of Lizbeth that he missed her footsteps on the kitchen floor.

"How's it going?"

He felt her breasts against his back when she slid her arms around his waist. Encouraged by her touch, Beau swung around in her embrace. "It's coming."

Slipping her leg between his, with her thigh pressed tightly to his dick, her eyes sparkled. "I meant the gumbo." She licked her lips in what he assumed was an intentional tease, then giggled as she felt the growing heat in his shorts.

"It's time to start the roux. Throw this in that big pot and get to stirring, please." Handing her the half stick of butter still wrapped in paper, he grazed the inside of her wrist. Catching sight of her rapid pulse in her tan neck, his gaze slid to the soft flesh of her breasts. Knowing how they would feel under his lips, Beau's erection started throbbing. "We could move this off the burner and take a little break."

Laughing, Liz's eyes shot to the clock. "Amy and Carolee will be here in less than ten minutes. If this morning is an example, neither of us will come that quickly."

He dropped his head in mock disappointment. "With a body like yours, you can't blame me for trying. I hope that you'll consider spending the night with me."

She kissed him on the cheek before pushing herself out of his embrace, fluttering her hand in front of herself. "Thank you for the compliment, sir. I do declare that you're spoiling my girls." Winking at him, she turned to the task of melting butter. "And, yes, I'd like that."

Beau poured the shrimp stock he'd created from the raw skins through a fine cheesecloth. Setting the solids aside, he stirred in the Cajun seasoning, along with thyme, bay leaves, and Worcestershire sauce into the broth. When Lizbeth had the butter melted, he sautéed the onions, then the peppers, celery, and garlic in the Dutch oven.

Enjoying the cooking comradery, he was a little let down when Liz's roommates arrived home in a whirlwind of excitement. But, as the three women laughed, teased and poked each other in the arms, he couldn't help but share in their infectious laughter.

"Hey, Beau. Which?" Amy was pointing at the wine cabinet.

"It's up to you. White is traditional with fish, but you can do a Pinot or Merlot with this."

"Alrighty. Both it is."

Beau found himself roaring with laughter as Amy

grabbed three bottles and left for the back porch, shouting over her shoulder. "Ladies, I'm parched!"

Twenty minutes later, after he'd reduced the gumbo to one simmering pot and put the rice on to cook, Beau moved outside to sit with Lizbeth and her friends. All three women wore big smiles and flushed cheeks, due in part to having nearly finished the first bottle of wine. But also, because Liz had been regaling them with her parasailing adventure. By the time dinner was ready, Amy was begging him and Liz to take her up with them. However, Beau noticed that Carolee was quietly staying out of any possible commitment to going.

As darkness filled the sultry summer evening, Amy and Carolee worked with Beau to clean up the back porch and kitchen while Lizbeth packed an overnight bag. Then, with a hug from both younger women, they left for his house on the beach.

## Chapter Eight

After another athletic night of satisfying sex, Lizbeth found herself greeting the morning sun on the master bedroom deck. But, for as much as she enjoyed spending time with Beau, she felt like he was hiding something from her. When he brought her morning coffee out, she watched his face closely.

"Tell me about Beau Landry." She saw his grip tighten on the mug he palmed.

"Well darlin', that's about fifty years-worth of story. Where do you want me to start?"

Reaching over to caress his forearm, Liz gave him free rein. "Wherever you want."

He chuckled deeply. "The short version is that I grew up in Charleston, where I have a business. I'm single and I like your company."

"Oh, Mr. Evasive. I prefer a novel over a Haiku." She saw his eyes flash. "How about a little more detail. Like, why you're in Myrtle Beach. Do you have family? Are you in the mob? Or a relationship?"

"Definitely no relationship."

She felt relief wash over her.

"But I can't really deny the mob connection."

And then was quickly dashed.

"Seriously, Lizbeth. You should see the look on your face." His booming laughter at her expense carried across the sandy beach. "Sorry, I'll give you the real stuff. But let me refill our coffee first."

Liz stood at the edge of the deck railing while Beau was inside. Despite her years in a classroom, patience was not her strong suit. She didn't want to be distracted right now. She wanted him to itemize a lifetime that she could be comfortable with. *But why? You're going back to New York in a few weeks.*

"Here's your coffee, darlin'."

Turning to look at her sexy, southerner lover when he spoke, she couldn't answer her own question. Returning to her teak chair, she mumbled a thank you and took the hot mug. Pretty soon the Myrtle Beach sun would make drinking it unbearable, but for now she found comfort in sipping the black nectar.

"Start with the mob thing." Lizbeth looked over her cup at Beau.

"Well, it was a joke. But I do come from a domineering background. My old man is an eighth-generation Charleston business man. And a tough, grizzled, old mean one at that." He took a deep swallow of coffee. "I am his only son, but I do have two sisters."

"What type of business?"

"Well, honestly it started out as moon-shining. But for obvious reasons, the Landry family had to come up with something more legitimate. The next couple generations took to fishing and started to dabble in good ol' southern politics. When my great-grandfather was at the helm, the whole thing had morphed into a one-stop supply house for restaurants."

Liz noted that Beau had yet to turn to her while he described his family history, causing her to wonder about his experience.

"By the time my father took over, every eating establishment, new and old, was buying exclusively from the Landry family. And I mean exclusively. Everything from furniture, linen, dishes, place settings, pots, pans, and even the appliances installed in their kitchens. Then, my old man expanded the empire by including booze."

"What part are you involved with?"

"Nothing directly in my father's company. Before my mom died, she'd already refereed enough business arguments between me and Montgomery Landry to know that I had inherited more of her personality than his. So, she insisted that I be paid out for my inheritance and allowed to build my own life, with one request."

Liz thought she heard contempt in his voice when he spoke of his father but continued to listen to Beau's story. "Momma insisted that I remain on the board of my father's company, ML Incorporated, and that he be on the board of anything new I created." She watched him cross the deck to lean on the railing, facing her. "A couple years after my mom died, my wife was killed in a car accident outside of Savannah. I had an eight-year old daughter and a struggling business that my father kept interfering with." Beau folded his arms across his bare chest, crushing the fine, blonde layer of hair. "I felt like I was circling the drain. It sucked."

She wanted badly to pull him into her arms, to kiss him, to sooth his past pain. But Lizbeth knew that Beau needed to finish his story.

"That was nearly twenty-one years ago. And me, Carli, and our company made it through."

When he returned to the chair next to her, Liz reached out to hold his hand. "Tell me about your daughter."

His face lit up at her request. "Carli's a beauty. And wicked smart. Holds an MBA and manages the product development side of Southerner's Folly with the proverbial iron fist." He laughed deeply. "Her nails are always nicely manicured, but that fist could blast you through a wall."

"What is it the company makes?" Given his upbringing, Lizbeth assumed it was in some way hospitality related.

"Dessert liquors made only from products grown in South Carolina." Another infectious smile filled his handsome features.

"You mean like peaches?" It was the only fruit she could think of as a confused look crossed her face.

"Peaches, sweet potatoes, watermelons, pecans, and even honey." He nodded at her. "You'd be amazed at how enjoyable an alcoholic version of honeyed sweet potatoes can be."

Beau rose from his chair, pulling Liz into his embrace. "Enough about me. Let's go inside and make some breakfast while I learn more about you." His lips teased her neck, raising goose bumps of excitement in the tender area below her ear. "Today is the last day of our extreme privacy. My house keeper will be back from vacation tomorrow." She felt her body deflate a little in his arms. "Darlin', don't be so let down. My lunchtime plan for you includes making you comfy on the rug in front of the fireplace and covering your body with some Sweet Potato Honey by Southerner's Folly, topped off with a most lickable layer of fresh whipped cream."

Lizbeth's mound pulsed with an instant surge of heat

as a low moan worked its way up her throat, making it hard to speak. "That sounds yummy for breakfast."

With a deep, knowing chuckle he nibbled on her ear lobe. "I'd prefer to have fruit to start my day. How about I bathe these beauties in some sweet peaches?"

Liz's back arched when he cupped her breasts, his thumbs crossing her nipples. "And maybe a little of our Sticky Pecan Praline can find it's way down here."

One of his hands slid inside her shorts to her vagina, deftly separating her lips and flicking across her clit. "There's a big ol' oak table downstairs that is perfect for you to lay that sexy ass down on."

She pressed against his teasing hand.

"I'm dying for something to eat. How about you?"

Enjoying his play on words almost as much as his flicking fingers, Lizbeth laughed boldly before stepping out of his embrace. "Simply starving." She walked a few feet and turned around, licking her lips. "Feed me Beau Landry." She fondled her breasts for emphasis. "Feed me."

BREAKFAST WAS as sticky and pleasurable as he had promised, requiring they shower before preparing actual food. When they finally sat at the freshly washed table to have steak and eggs, it was time for Lizbeth to give him some details about her life.

"It's your turn to spill." Beau rubbed her forearm while she took a deep breath.

"I'm afraid it isn't as romantic as your past." She looked down at his hand resting on her arm. "I'm an only child, fifty-two, widowed with no children, and I've spent my whole life telling people two things." She held up her right index finger. "One. No, I did not speak so quickly that I slurred the letters. My name is not Elizabeth." Up popped another digit. "Two. I always wanted to be a teacher. Both of my parents were, and it's all I ever dreamed of."

Beau leaned back in his chair, giving her space to deliver what she needed to.

"As you can tell, I'm taller than most women. I'm a former athlete who has always preferred being outdoors to anything inside. Anytime I could, I'd take my students outside and teach in the park near the school, especially if it was science or art."

He watched her smile fade a little.

"My late husband, Jim, and I did everything together. You name it: running, hiking, travel, boating." She stopped her litany to look out at the beach. "He died on our sailboat, two years ago."

The sadness in her voice tugged at Beau. "I'm sorry. That's not very long ago."

"You don't have to be sorry. You know what it's like to lose a spouse." Her voice had developed a steely edge.

"Lizbeth, that was a long time ago. I was only nineteen when I found out I was going to be a dad and twenty-seven when Carli's mom died. I've had time to heal."

"I'm getting there." When she looked at him, a light shimmer of tears pooled in her eyes. "Amy and Carolee had to bully and bamboozle me into coming on this trip with them." Her long fingers lightly stroked Beau's lips. "But I'm glad they did."

"What happened to Jim?"

She cast her eyes to the sea, speaking in a monotone. "We had dropped anchor the night before in the north end of Lake George, about five-hundred yards off Roger's Rock. It was the perfect summer night to be out on the water. Jim had made fresh shrimp scampi while I pulled together a salad. A deep red sunset gave way to a full moon, which we enjoyed with a few local amber ales, listening to the loons serenade us from the north shore. After making love, we fell asleep to the gentle rocking of the boat."

Liz continued to stare at the water. "It was very early, like, just breaking dawn when I felt him kiss me and get out of bed. But I'd taken two anti-histamines the night before, so I fell back to sleep immediately. When I finally woke, the sun was in my face. I got up to see where he was. It was weird. There was no coffee, no obvious signs that he'd made breakfast, and the dingy was floating in the water off the stern."

Beau's skin puckered in fear for what Lizbeth would say next. Watching her withdrawn expression, he wasn't sure if sharing each other's story had been a good idea.

"When I crossed under the jib to stand on the pulpit, I looked down over the side of the bow. And there he was. One of his legs was caught in the extra rope from the anchor and the upper half of his body was submerged under water."

"Oh, Liz." Beau pulled her into his arms as a deep sob tore from her chest, her shoulders shaking uncontrollably.

"I couldn't help him, he was too heavy. I tried pulling on the rope but all it did was tear my hands. And I couldn't stop screaming. Someone on shore must have heard me, 'cause a small motorboat came rushing across the water."

Beau's heart ached for her as tears cascaded to the floor.

"And then the cops and the other medical people came on board. It was chaos and all I could do was sit by myself below deck while they pulled my husband out of the water."

With her face buried in his shoulder, Beau felt when she finally got her jagged breath under control.

Pulling from his arms, she sat down and continued.

"At first it was considered a questionable death. But my toxicology report showed the extra anti-histamine and his autopsy came back as a drowning. So, they ruled it an accident and left me to go about my life. A life that had died in the cold, northern water of Lake George."

Beau waited a moment to see if she was finished.

"Yesterday was the first time I've been on a boat since then." With that final statement, Liz stood from the table and walked to the wall of windows facing the Atlantic Ocean. After a few minutes she returned to Beau's side and kissed his cheek. "Thank you."

"For what?" In shock, he stared at her swollen face.

"For showing me how to laugh again. To live again. For listening. No one else knows the full story about his death. Not even Amy and Carolee."

This time, Beau pulled her into his lap, her tight derriere pressing against his parts, warming them into action. "I think a change of scenery is in order. Can the girls survive without you for a few days?"

"Um, probably. Why?"

"I need to make a trip to Aiken to meet with a few of the farmers handling this year's sweet potato crop."

Lizbeth tipped her head with a puzzled expression.

"Have you been to the South Carolina hill country?" He felt a smile on his own face as she shook her head. Nudging her from his lap, he stood and wrapped her in his arms. "We'll leave in the morning. Tell Amy and Carolee you'll be back on Wednesday for dinner."

Leaning her back so he could enjoy the deep green of her eyes, Beau wanted desperately to make love to Lizbeth. But, he thought she needed a few hours to rest after her emotional confession. "For now, let's take a walk on the beach before that thunderstorm arrives." He pointed to the large black clouds rolling into the northern sky.

Hand in hand, they crossed the sand to the where the surf had made it hard-packed. As the swelling in her face faded, Liz seemed to have let go of the sadness that had engulfed her earlier as she filled him in on the professional side of her life. Having grown up in Albany, and attended college there, she started working at the public high school in a clerical job while in college. When she finished her master's degree and started teaching, she was able to buy back the previous time. And, even though she was only fifty-two, she had well over thirty years of service and could, in theory, retire with a full pension.

*Wait. Meaning she could move if she wanted to? She could be down here with him?* Beau shocked himself with that thought. Why would she be interested in leaving her life up north?

"You didn't tell me why you have a house in Myrtle Beach. Why do you?" She tugged on his hand with the question, pulling him out of his daydreaming.

"At first it was just an investment to piss off my father. He considers Myrtle Beach to be a tacky back water with no heritage. Nothing but the respectable gentility of Charleston will do for Montgomery Landry." Beau barked with laughter when he realized that he'd described his father like something out of *Gone with the Wind*. "I enjoyed designing it and overseeing the construction. All three stories are a part of my personality and I like being there."

"Are you on vacation?"

"What? Oh, no. More like I'm hiding out." He saw Lizbeth's brows furrow and remembered what she'd said to him the day before '*Always honestly.*' "A few months ago, a woman from the Charleston area claimed I was the father of her unborn child. Now, because I've had a vasectomy, that couldn't possibly be true. But due to my family's wealth, and that I had dated her a few times, it's making for great tabloid fodder in the area."

"Dated or had sex?" Lizbeth was, if nothing else, very direct.

"Both. But, mostly sex. Until I figured out that she was more interested in my bank account than she was my anatomy. So, I broke it off and about a month later, the rumors started swirling."

"Does she have a name?"

"Yes, Josie Fitch. Of the Savannah Fitch family"

Liz laughed in response. "I don't know much about southern dynasties."

"All you need to know is that I challenged her to a DNA test, but she's been pretty cagey about that. My daughter and I decided that I should lay low in "tourist town USA" until the clucking old gossips of Charleston figure out that Ms. Fitch is obviously over-eating, and lying, because she's been pregnant for over ten months."

Suddenly, his statement ended with a natural exclamation point when a bolt of lightning dropped to the water. The nearly instant and deafening thunder that followed had Beau and Lizbeth racing down shore for the safety of his house as the warm rain instantly saturated them.

## Chapter Nine

For Lizbeth, the trip across South Carolina had been exceptional. Not only had Beau been quite generous in explaining the intricacies of cultivating raw agricultural products through to the delectable finished beverages sold by his company, but he'd done it with laughter. Regardless of how many questions she asked, he'd smile while answering—never once making her feel inferior in her lack of knowledge.

The two nights were spent in hotels resplendent with southern detail and charm. And, somewhere between the salt air of the beach and the rolling hills of Aiken, their intimacy had shifted from two people having flaming, hot sex to a trusting couple expressing passion and respect for each other.

Still wrestling with this new set of emotions, Liz was happy to return to Myrtle Beach to see her friends. But, she was very surprised to find them home during the day.

"No air conditioning, so school's closed for a few days." Carolee came in from the back porch when Liz and Beau walked into the kitchen.

"We've got time to play," Amy yelled from the laundry room. "What do you want to do?"

"Okay, so this is unexpected." Liz was caught off guard. "Any idea how long it'll be?"

"No. So we have to stay somewhere in Myrtle Beach in case they call us in." Amy stood in front of her, pouting.

Liz wasn't sure how to proceed. In the past two weeks she'd spent so much time with Beau that she'd forgotten about the original list of ideas they'd drawn up on the road trip from Albany. She felt his hand on her shoulder. "Lizbeth, I'm going to leave you ladies to this."

Turning to protest, she caught the look of desperation on Amy's face. "Sure. Thanks for showing me Aiken."

"Any time, doll." He kissed her forehead. "Call me tonight if you find time. I'll let myself out."

After he left, Carolee sprinted from the room mumbling something about maps and Amy plopped down into one of the chairs at the kitchen table. "I'm so glad you're home."

"I know we're buds and all, but Carolee's just not as much fun as you are. And her man friend doesn't begin to be as hot." Amy burst out laughing as she made a sizzling sound while touching her finger to her own arm.

"Alright, let's focus on something to do." Liz's cheeks filled with heat at the thought of how down right scorching Beau's body truly was and what he did to hers. "Carolee, where are you?"

"Here." Carolee's curls bounced happily as she trotted back into the room to hand a stack of random papers to Lizbeth. "The list of ideas. Coupons. Maps."

"Here. Let's try this one since it's right around the corner." Liz held up the advertising flyer for Gator Greens. "Apparently, it's an animal park showcasing a wide range of swamp species." The hair on her neck rose at the idea of slithering creatures, but she knew her friends would like it. With any luck, most of the crawling things would be stuffed and mounted.

"Alright! Maybe a 'gator will attack somebody while we're there." Amy was laughing as she grabbed her purse and headed to the garage. "I'll start the car, somebody lock the front door."

Four hours later, as the friends dropped themselves into a booth at the delightfully airconditioned Crab-a-nation, they were hot and sweaty, but laughing. Not only had the alligators at Gator Greens been very much alive, but so were all of their distant relatives that wandered freely in and out of countless brackish water pits, gnashing their teeth at each other. From her perspective, Lizbeth couldn't believe the liability of having known razor-toothed amphibians loose with people. But watching the reaction of the people around them had been priceless.

Returning to the house as a deep golden sunset bathed the western sky, Liz thought of Beau, suppressing the urge to call him.

After all three had showered, the women retreated to the privacy of the back porch with wine in hand. Two glasses in, Carolee began confessing about her time spent with the grocery store Casanova, blushing profusely when Amy asked direct questions about sex. Based upon how easily Carolee answered her, the two had been down this path before.

But, for as much as she appreciated the support and friendship of these two, Liz was pleased that neither woman had pried too deeply about her time spent with Beau. Ever since their confessional day, Lizbeth felt a strong bond growing with him. A wonderful excitement, a new closeness that was more than just the life-altering sex they'd been having. And, she wasn't ready to share that with anyone.

As the house was wrapped in the dark summer night, Liz excused herself for the evening, feigning fatigue.

"Say good night to Beau for me," Amy shouted as Lizbeth quietly closed her bedroom door.

When school was cancelled for a second day, the room-mates decided to explore two new areas: T.I.G.E.R.S. Preservation Station—a wildlife habitat for big cats and other animals—and the Russell Burgess Coastal Preserve. Since T.I.G.E.R.S. was farther away, they opted for that to be the first stop.

Shortly after breakfast, all three piled into Amy's car in pursuit of lions, cheetahs, elephants, ligers, and chim-panzees. As far as Lizbeth could tell, they were in for another sweaty day around dirty, wild creatures. She hoped for materials to bring back to her classroom in Albany.

By late afternoon, the three friends were freshly sunburned and realized the Coastal Preserve would have to wait for another day. With full consensus, they returned to the house long enough to pull on bathing suits and headed to the beach, with every intention of staying submerged in the water until their skin turned to prunes.

Later that night, disappointment swamped Liz when she spoke to Beau. She'd been telling him about their day holding baby animals, feeding them bottles of milk, and scratching behind their ears when he abruptly cut her off.

"Look, Lizbeth. Can we talk about this some other time?" When she didn't respond, he kept talking. "You're prattling about play time, but I've got a big business problem that I'm working on with my daughter. I'll stop by and see you tomorrow night."

Feeling chastised, Liz mumbled an apology, discon-nected the call and climbed into bed. For the first time in weeks, the grip of loneliness travelled up her body, filling her chest and making it hard to breath while tears saturated her pillow.

"MORNING, LIZBETH." Amy was waiting on the back porch when Liz finally found the strength to get out of bed. It had taken her hours to fall asleep. Between the heat of her sunburn and the unending tears, she had been in agony. And then, like all good tormentors are wont to do, Beau arrived in her dreams. One minute lifting her body to new levels of ecstasy, the next yelling at her about having no sense of business. Sometime around seven, Liz awoke to her body covered in a glistening sheen of sweat and her legs trapped in her sheets and a miniature man jackhammering in her head. It had to be a man, women didn't do asshole things like that.

"Hey." She avoided Amy's gaze and sat facing the yard.

"You look like shit. Did you get any sleep?" Her friend's statement made her smile.

"Not much. Must have been the sunburn. Is school closed again?"

"Yeah and probably just as well. Carolee's snoring up a storm. She's going to wake up with a doozey of a hangover." Amy laughed at their friend's expense. "I guess we'll hang here this morning and go to the preserve after lunch."

"Good idea." Liz stood and walked to the door. "I'm going back to bed. If I'm not moving by eleven, make some noise." She smiled at Amy and retreated to her room to hide for a few more hours.

Shortly before lunch, Liz found the younger women sitting in the living room with their feet propped up, watching television. "Hey, I can make that," Carolee shouted at Amy.

"Like hell you can. Carolee, you can't even boil water. Why do you think Liz has been cooking for us? I'm afraid you'll poison me by accident." Amy's insult earned her a punch in the arm.

"Are you guys ready to head out?"

Amy shut off the television and bounced to her feet. "Yep, just waiting for you."

Carolee grunted slightly as she lifted her fuller figure from the overstuffed furniture. "Never date a grocery guy, he brings home too many cookies and cakes." She laughed at herself while tugging down her shirt.

In what was becoming their standard travel banter, the women drove Amy's car to the northern part of Myrtle Beach to find the Russell Burgess Coastal Preserve. Since they'd arrived at low tide, Lizbeth considered the area to look like a swamp. Wrinkling her nose at the brackish, pungent smell of swampy earth that rose from the thick mud, she wondered why people were enamored by the place.

But, there was a newer boardwalk several feet above the water, wrapping through the trees and tall grass allowing them to meander. Staring into the afternoon sun, Liz blinked a few times, thinking she was seeing something in the sand. She pointed to an area by a large, corrugated drainage pipe. "What's that?"

Amy leaned on the railing and laughed. "Oh my gosh, you need glasses. Hermit crabs."

As the sand started to shift, Lizbeth realized that it wasn't just one crab—it was hundreds, moving inland. She was mesmerized. Each time the water fluctuated from the incoming tide, a wave of the crabs retreated, hastily running over each other in their quest for safety.

Tiring of that, the women walked under an arch of flowering trees and around the corner to find a thin, older man standing in the deep mud, pulling something across the surface.

"Excuse me, sir." Liz waited until he looked up at her. "Are you trying to catch something?"

"Yes, ma'am. Blue crabs." He nodded politely at her.

"What kind of bait is that?"

"It's greasy chicken back. The crabs love it. They feel the pressure on the mud and come out top to try to grab it from me. That's when I snag 'em with my net and bucket 'em."

After spending so much time with Beau, Lizbeth had no trouble understanding this man's thick drawl. "So, only in low tide?"

"That's right, ma'am. The water's starting to come up now and they can feel it, that's why they're deep in the mud."

When Amy grabbed her arm to leave, Liz smiled at the crabber as she left. "Thank you, sir."

He waved with his free hand.

They took the boardwalk deep into the preserve, snapping pictures of every plant, bird, and bug they could find, laughing about it being an occupational hazard when educators were someplace new. On their return, Lizbeth noticed the fisherman had left and wondered how many he'd caught.

As they approached the flowering tree arch, Carolee dropped to her knees in a quivering pile of humanity, pointing over her head.

"Carolee, what's wrong." Liz reached her first, placing her hand on Carolee's shoulder.

"Look up." She rolled her shoulders defensively. "I. I. I

can't go through there. Oh my god, how am I getting out of here?"

When Liz raised her eyes, she had to suppress her own scream. *Good god almighty. Look at those things!* Her skin crawled at the site of countless numbers of huge yellow spiders suspended in webs. *Where did they come from?* Liz dropped to her knees in sympathy to Carolee.

"Ha ha ha ha…you guys look like scare-dee cats." Amy mocked them. "They're just spiders. And news flash, you already walked under them once."

Her ruthless laugh echoed in Lizbeth's ears as she and Carolee scampered to safety on their hands and knees. When they got past the arbor, she stood up, dragging Carolee with her. When they reached Amy, Lizbeth gave her the finger, with both hands.

"Ha ha ha ha. I wish I'd taken a picture. Wait until the whole school hears about this." Still laughing, Amy waited for them at the car.

Traveling back to their house, Carolee gave up her anger, chatting endlessly with Amy. But not Liz, she was hunkered in for a long pout. First Beau's insults, now Amy's mockery. She was cranky. Deep in her self-indulgent stew, Lizbeth was only half seeing her surroundings until she realized that they were stopped in traffic across the street from Alto Presco, the beachy fusion restaurant where she and Beau went on their first date.

Trying to ignore the pangs in her heart, Liz looked away. But a laughing couple, their arms wrapped around each other while coming down the front steps drew her attention. Beau. It was Beau! Holding a beautiful young blonde. When they stopped at the sidewalk, his head pitched back in exuberant laughter at something she said.

Liz grabbed at her throat, unable to breath. *And I believed him about the woman from Charleston. About the DNA test and everything. And here he is, laughing with her, holding her in broad daylight.* Like watching a car accident, she couldn't tear her eyes from the carnage, watching as Beau lead the leggy young thing to her car, opening the door for her, kissing her forehead before she slipped inside. As the woman drove off, Beau looked around, his eyes landing on Amy's car as it started to move in traffic. Lizbeth saw him raise his arm as she covered her eyes to hide the silent tears that were running down her cheeks.

A few hours later, Lizbeth heard a soft knock on her bedroom door, but didn't respond.

"Liz?" It was Amy. "Liz, Beau's here."

"I don't want to see him."

"Liz, he's standing on the front stoop. What do you want me to say to him?"

Enraged by Amy's muffled voice, Liz crossed the room in a few brisk steps and yanked the door open. "Tell him to take his cheating ass and get the hell away from me." Without addressing the shocked look on her friend's face, she slammed the door as hard as she could and locked it. Then, she picked up her cell phone and shut it off so he couldn't reach her.

She had no idea what Amy said to get him off the front stoop, but she didn't care. She'd spent the rest of the night locked in seclusion, wishing she had a bottle of wine to drink herself into a stupor. The next day she heard the younger women leave for work, thankful she had the house to herself. When they returned, neither asked questions. Instead, they kept her company on the back porch, drinking wine well into the next day. Fortunately for them, it was Saturday.

## Chapter Ten

Three days had passed since she'd felt the stab wounds Beau had given her heart. When she had finally turned her phone back on, she was inundated with voicemails and text messages from him. In his defense, he sounded sad and confused. But she couldn't give in. Not even to the last message. The one where his voice dropped to a soft whisper, telling her how much he missed her and needed to see her.

"Bullshit!"

She yelled loudly as her legs pumped wildly on her bike. After several days of doing nothing but sitting, eating, and drinking, it felt great to have her muscles work. Even if it was to burn off the intense anger and aggression she'd built up. The late morning sun baked her sweat glistened skin as she pulled up to a stop light on south Ocean Boulevard. Watching the beachgoers cross her path, she didn't notice the runner coming up beside her. As the light turned green, Liz stood on the raised right pedal to push off when she caught a glimpse of the large masculine figure a few feet away. Beau. *God, Liz. What were you thinking? His house is only a few blocks from here.*

"Lizbeth!"

Chastising herself internally, she pumped as hard as she could to escape his shouts. Sweat drenched her face, rolling into her eyes. The blinding salt made it hard to see. And she could still hear him shouting her name. Liz tried to wipe her eyes with her right hand, for a split-second closing both of them at the same time. Just as she opened them, a small sedan backed out of a driveway, directly in her path. Liz slammed the break in her left hand, causing the bike to jackknife and send her flying over the hot surface of the older car. Agonizing pain filled her back and legs when she crashed to the asphalt curb on the other side.

"Lizbeth!" Beau was still shouting her name when she felt his hands lift her from the street. "Oh my god, are you okay?" She let his hands travel her body, until she remembered how angry she was with him.

Slapping his bare chest as hard as she could, Lizbeth stepped into the street, ignoring the gathering crowd. "Get your hands off me!" she screeched in his direction. "You dirty bastard."

Liz heard sirens, coming closer, then saw the police car flying toward her on South Ocean Boulevard. She spun, slightly off balance, to look for her bike. She needed to get away from Beau. She hadn't done anything wrong and didn't need the police. Picking up her bike, she righted her helmet and moved into the street just as the cruiser came to a stop, it's red lights flashing in her eyes.

"Ma'am. Are you okay? Do you need an ambulance?"

Leaning heavily on her handle bar, Liz shook her head. "No, officer. I'm fine. Can I go?"

He looked at her skeptically, pointing to the blood on her lower legs. "Are you sure?'

Starting to walk away from him, Liz pushed her bike through the milling people. "Yes, I'm fine." Without another word, she walked a few more feet before swinging her leg over the seat to remount, just as a hand covered hers.

"Lizbeth, please. Don't do this." Beau's deep voice shook. "If you won't go to the hospital, at least come to my house so I can help you clean those wounds."

Liz looked down at her quivering, burning legs. Gravel and dirt were matted to them and blood was pooling in her socks. She wasn't even sure she had the strength to ride home. Admitting defeat internally, she looked at Beau. "Okay. But only for a minute."

WITHOUT SPEAKING, Beau walked with Lizbeth for the two blocks to his house. When he offered to take her bicycle, she had declined and moved it between them, effectively keeping him at a safe distance. He couldn't figure out what he had done for her to push him away like this. Less than a week ago they had been in Aiken, admiring the quaint southern city, marveling at the horseback riding trail system that wound in and out of the public parks. She'd been so taken by the massive oak trees, with their dripping Spanish moss. But now, leaning heavily on the bike and limping, she wouldn't look at him.

When they reached his front yard, Beau suggested she let him carry the bike up the long, sweeping staircase to the door, promising he'd leave it on the porch for when she was ready to go. She seemed to be assessing her options, then nodded silently. After letting go of the bike, Lizbeth moved to the broad white banister and slowly climbed to the top. Her pain was evident, but Beau was afraid to ask about the location, fearing he'd trigger an angry outburst.

Once inside, he pointed across the bright room to the kitchen. "Grab a seat, I'll get the first aid stuff." Without waiting, he ducked into the first-floor bathroom, coming out with a large plastic toolbox and a pill bottle. Pouring a large glass of ice water, he slid the drink and the pills in front of her. "Naproxen."

Mumbling her thank you, Lizbeth swallowed two of the blue pills and half the glass of water. "I know. You're only supposed to take one at a time." She still wouldn't meet his gaze. "My liver will have to buck up. I want the pain to go away."

"Looks like your lower right side took most of the hit."

In silent response, she ran her fingers over her rapidly swelling knee.

Beau stepped to the sink, to soak a clean wash cloth in warm water. Turning back, he squatted in front of her. "Let's get the blood and dirt out of everything first, then I'll get you an ice pack." Since she didn't protest, he began cleaning her wounds. From the corner of his eye, he could see Lizbeth biting her lip, but she still didn't make a sound.

Once he had her leg clean, he ran his hand down the back of her calf, caressing the round muscle before stopping just above her ankle. "I need to take these off." He started to unlace the sneaker with one hand while supporting her injured leg with the other. Then he peeled the blood-soaked sock and dropped it in the dirt and debris that had fallen from her body. To distract her, he massaged the ball of her foot while he looked at the deep gash he'd just revealed. *There must have been a piece of metal or glass next to the curb.*

"That's a pretty good cut you gave yourself." This time

she looked at him, but he couldn't place the emotion he saw floating in her eyes. "The good news is, it bled so much that you probably don't have to worry about tetanus or an infection."

Beau cleaned around the wound before standing up. When he saw Lizbeth start to rise, he placed his hand on her shoulder. "Stay put until I pour some peroxide over everything." He heard her deep sigh, but at least she hadn't pulled away from his touch. Ten minutes later, she was holding a cold pack as she hobbled to the couch. "Rest a bit while I clean up the kitchen." She took his hand for support as she lowered herself down, keeping the weight off her injured leg. Once she was comfortable, Beau slipped the light-weight afghan over her lean but battered frame before crossing the large expanse to tidy up. A few minutes later, her breathing slowed, telling him she had fallen asleep.

LOST IN WORK, Beau wasn't sure how long Lizbeth had slept when he felt her delicate, long fingers touch his cheek.

"I don't care who she was." Her voice was soft, almost apologetic. Pushing back from his desk, he turned to look up at her.

"Who?"

"The woman I saw you kissing outside our restaurant." She looked at the floor instead of his eyes.

"Lizbeth, what are you talking about?" His mind scrambled to make sense of what she was saying. Then, he remembered.

"Are you talking about the other day when you guys passed Alto Presco?"

Still hiding her emotions, she nodded.

Slowly, Beau rose from the padded leather chair. Cupping her face, he tilted her chin so that he could see the deep green of her eyes. "Lizbeth, that was my daughter."

She blinked at him for a second.

"Carli had come up to show me blueprints for the new tasting area we're building in the fall."

He watched a storm of emotions roll through her eyes, the green going darker and then settling at hazel as they filled with tears. "Lizbeth, please listen to me. It was Carli. I would never cheat on you. Ever since I met you, I can't think straight when we're apart." With his thumb, Beau wiped away the single tear that escaped. Waiting for her to speak, he focused on her lips. Those soft, plump lips that had brought unspeakable pleasure to his body. Those lips, that he'd missed deeply in the past few days. Leaning down, he grazed them lightly with his own and then pulled away.

"Lizbeth, there is no other…" He hadn't finished the sentence when her mouth crashed into his, her tongue commanding him to open, to let her in. With her arms wrapped tightly around his neck, Liz's chest heaved against his as the kiss deepened, igniting a firestorm of need in Beau's body.

Nearly breathless, Lizbeth's hands slipped down his arm until she had his hands. Withdrawing from their kiss, she looked at him, licking her lower lip. "I want you."

"But, you're injured." He tried resisting as she pulled him to the door of his office.

"Not where I need you the most." He watched the green swirling tempest in her eyes as she slid her hand down his abdomen and cupped his manhood.

Staggered by his own need, Beau followed her to his bed without further argument.

BEAU LET the powerful jets of water hammer his muscles. Never in his wildest imagination did he think he'd be complaining about too much sex, especially after several days of missing her. But Lizbeth had been a demanding fiend from the moment they stepped into the bedroom— almost as if she had a split personality.

Stripping off her clothes, first she ordered him to his knees, his face level with her burning need. Her fingers locked in his hair, forcing his face into her snatch until she was dripping with desire. Then, on the bed, she'd positioned them so she could be on top without causing further injury to her leg and ankle. And, she'd ridden him nonstop for what seemed like an hour, her grinding hips forcing him deeply inside while his stomach muscles struggled to thrust. When she exploded in her fifth orgasm, he gave up on discipline and let his own fly. After which, they both passed out in a tangle of arms, legs, and sweaty sheets.

He felt the draft of cool air before her arms wrapped around him, her breasts pressing against his back. "Hi beautiful."

Lizbeth nuzzled him before reaching for a bar of soap. "Where are we going for dinner?" Her question confused him, so he turned to look at her.

"I thought you said you wanted to stay in?"

Her eyes clouded for a second as she shook her head. "No. I want to go out. You said I can drive." During their trip to Aiken, Liz had enjoyed the smooth handling of his Mercedes, doing most of the driving on the way home.

"Okay. How about Alto Presco?" Beau kissed her lightly and stepped out of the shower, leaving her some privacy. "I'll be waiting downstairs for you."

Twenty minutes later, they left the house with Lizbeth

behind the wheel, wearing an outfit she'd left at his house weeks before. Laughing, she fiddled with the radio, stopping when Sade's sultry voice filled the car. Then she reached across the console to tease him, rubbing his package. "Looks like you're ready for some fun."

Beau couldn't deny that he was already reacting to her touch. "After the romp we just had, I can't believe this." He lifted her hand from his lap.

"What do you mean? What romp? We haven't had sex since that grand hotel in Aiken."

*What the hell? My dick feels like she wore the skin right off of it.* Beau felt his brows furrow. "Babe, you're gonna miss the turn." Lizbeth frowned at him as he pointed to the restaurant. "Here. Turn right. The parking lot is in the back."

Liz pulled into a spot in the last row and looked around a moment. "What are we doing here?"

"What?" Beau felt like she was playing some sort of game. "First you don't want to go out, then you do. I suggested this restaurant because you like it. And now you're questioning why we're here?"

"I'm not hungry for food. I just want to go home and have sex." She rubbed his crotch for emphasis.

"Lizbeth, we just had sex. A lot of sex." He tried to keep from shouting, but, was losing control. "Almost an hour's worth of hot, grinding sex. You were such an animal that you almost put my back out."

She looked out the window again, responding with a slight tremor in her voice. "I don't know where we are."

As a feeling of dread came over him, Beau slipped out of the car and moved around to the driver's side, opening the door. "Here, baby. Take my hand." Liz cooperated as he led her to stand by the car. "Lizbeth, follow my finger and do what I do."

118

Watching his finger travel back and forth, she giggled when they each touched their nose.

"What's six plus six?"

She tipped her head in question. "Twelve. Why?"

"Where'd be have dinner on our first date?"

A big smile crossed her face. "Crab-a-nation. By the alligator place."

*What the hell is Crab-a-nation?* Beau's sense of dread exploded into full blow fear. Worried that she was having a stroke, he turned her gently, leading her to the passenger's side of his car. "Darlin', I'm going to drive for a while." Once she was settled, he dashed around the SUV to get behind the steering wheel. But instead of going north, Beau headed south on Route 17 to the get to the closest hospital.

"Lizbeth, where's your phone?"

She pulled it from her purse and waved it at him. "Okay, call Amy or Carolee and tell them to meet us at the Grand Strand Medical Center. It's just off 17."

A small piece of Beau shattered when he saw her hands shaking. She greeted Amy and then turned to him. "She wants to know why."

He pulled to the shoulder so that he could turn to face Liz. Placing his hand on her arm, he strove for calm, but it was a challenge. "Babe, there's something wrong with you. I don't know what, but you're not acting like yourself. So, I'm taking you to the hospital. Now tell Amy to meet us there and bring any medications you have at the house."

After relaying the information to Amy, Lizbeth sat in her seat, motionless except for the way she was worrying her lower lip. Beau wished she would speak so he could monitor her pattern, but she didn't respond to his simple banter. He knew he said a few internal thank you's when the blue and white hospital sign came into view. Then, he said a few more when he saw her friends racing across the Emergency Room parking lot. Tightlipped, Amy carried a small canvas bag; Carolee's face was blotched and red. If either of them was surprised to see him with Lizbeth, they didn't say it.

With an odd serenity, she met with the triage nurse, supplying what seemed like critical medical information. When they took her to an exam room, she insisted there was nothing wrong but placated them by changing into a hospital gown. After the ER nurse went through her vitals, she pointed to the abrasions on Liz's right leg.

"Looks like you took a nasty spill. When did that happen?"

Liz looked at her leg and shrugged. "Beats me."

The nurse turned to the rest of them squeezed into the small cubicle. First, she queried the roommates, but since it had just happened that day, neither of them were of help. Her accusing eyes fell to Beau. "Well?"

"It happened about five hours ago on South Ocean Boulevard. A car backed out in front of her while she was riding her bike. She refused an ambulance but was willing to limp the few blocks to my house to get cleaned up."

Amy squinted at him, apparently unsure of his story, but she didn't challenge him.

The nurse turned to Lizbeth, gently touching her hand. "The attending wants to do a few tests. We'll start with some x-rays and a CT scan. Okay?"

Beau saw Liz nod to the nurse before turning to her friends. "I'll be back." She attempted a mocking Terminator voice as she got wheeled from the small space.

The next several hours proved to be exhausting to everyone but Liz. While she was undergoing a barrage of tests, Beau brought Amy and Carolee up to speed, leaving out the intimacy they shared. Shortly after Liz was

120

returned to them, a man and woman wearing crisp, mono-grammed lab coats motioned him away from the bed, closing the curtain behind him.

"Mr. Landry, we'd like you to fill us in on Ms. Spensor's day. And we mean everything."

"I—I don't know how she spent her morning. I first saw her around noon. I was about two blocks short of finishing my run when she stopped at a red-light on her bicycle. She was covered in sweat and breathing hard. I hadn't seen her in a few days, so I shouted to her. But she took off like a crazy thing, pumping like mad on the bike. And then, a car shot backwards out into the street, right in front of her." Beau paused for a second remembering the fear in his heart when he saw Lizbeth fly across the front of the car. "She must have jammed her front brake 'cause the bike jackknifed and sent her over the hood of the car. When I got to her, she was trying to stand up. She refused help from the cop who showed up, or an ambulance. But I finally got her to agree to coming to my house to clean up. Then she took a nap for about an hour while I worked in my office."

"Go on." The woman's voice was gentle.

"What makes you think there's more?" Beau felt his face flush. The last thing he wanted to do was tell these perfect strangers about the incredible sex he and Lizbeth had shared earlier.

"We're doctors, Mr. Landry, not your minister. We're just looking for answers as to why a seemingly healthy woman is having memory issues. Did something else happen after she took a nap?" The man wasn't as comforting to Beau as the female neurologist had been. "Did you have sex?"

Beau started to deny the question, but caught the stern look both doctors gave him. "Yes."

"Was there something unusual about it?"

*Christ, what a perv this guy is.* "Lizbeth was a little more aggressive than usual." He felt both sets of eyes drilling a hole in him, but neither spoke. "Okay, yes. She was out of control. Like an animal, practically driving my ass right through the mattress. It was exhausting." He stretched his neck, hoping that Amy and Carolee hadn't heard his confession.

"Sir, we think Lizbeth has had a T.G.A." Beau blinked at the acronym. "Transient Global Amnesia occurs in women in their fifties. Basically, it's sudden and temporary loss of memory that cannot be blamed on other neurological issues such as a stroke. While the patient has a grasp of important details like their name, address, and people close to them, they can't remember recent events, or even the here and now."

Beau felt like his head was about to explode as the doctor continued. "This is a pretty vague area of study and very difficult to diagnose. But in the past, people who experience a TGA have reported one of these triggers happening just before the episode."

"What triggers?" Beau wasn't sure he wanted to know the answer, but the doctor ripped through a list.

"Mild head trauma, medical procedures like an endoscopy, sudden immersion in cold or hot water, strenuous physical activity, and sexual intercourse. It seems to me that you and Ms. Sponsor have the last two items covered."

Beau rolled his head, trying to relieve some of the tension in his neck. The female neurologist placed her hand on his arm before speaking. "Transient global amnesia isn't serious, but it is frightening. She hasn't come back to full memory yet, so we'd like to have her admitted."

He nodded as he pointed to the curtain a few feet away. "It's up to the three of them, but thanks for telling me all this privately." The woman smiled and turned to open the curtain. *Oh boy, it's show time.* Beau suppressed a grin when Amy spun around after the doctors gave their diagnosis, knowing that Lizbeth would never be able to keep this a secret when they returned to Albany.

# Epilogue

By the end of her first week of home-bound medical incarceration, even though Lizbeth was crazy with boredom, she had yet to resolve her fears over what happened. All week she tried to fit the pieces together but each time something was missing.

*When she "came to" in the hospital, she found Beau standing at the foot of the bed, grinning, while Amy and Carolee flanked either side, their hands resting on the railing. They asked her ridiculous questions that they should have known the answers to: What city were they in? Why were they there? How did she feel about using public bathrooms?*

*Then, Beau leaned forward and placed his hands on the blanket covering her feet. "Lizbeth. Where did we have dinner on our first date?"*

*"That's a crazy question."*

*"What's the answer?" He squeezed her toes just slightly.*

*"Alto Presco. Why?"*

*But before he could answer, Amy and Carolee burst into excited clapping and high-fived each other across the hospital bed.*

*"Yeah baby, she's back!" Amy's deep voice was laced with unmistakable joy.*

*"What do you mean? And why am I laying in this bed, wearing an awful nightgown thingy with this wristband on?"*

*"Lizbeth, you are never going to believe this." Carolee covered her mouth as her sentence turned into laughter.*

*Thoroughly confused, Liz looked at each friend and then at Beau, whose tanned, handsome face was a shade darker from a deep blush. "Will one of you please tell me what's going on?"*

Thinking back, Liz found her own face heating with embarrassment as she continued to replay the scene in her head. In short, she'd had the best sex of her life but couldn't remember any of it. The most she could grab onto were fleeting vignettes: crying tears of overwhelming happiness when Beau explained who the woman was that he'd been hugging four days before; she vaguely recalled driving his Mercedes on Route 17; calling Amy from the car when Beau had insisted they switch drivers; and then sitting silently with fear so great that she could barely breathe, let alone respond to Beau's chatter.

When she was discharged from the hospital two days after her "incident", Amy and Carolee had appeared to be thrilled when Beau offered that she stay with him, thereby having her supervised round the clock. She wanted to argue that she was not an errant child and didn't need to be coddled. But, the entire episode had shaken her self-confidence and, in some ways, she liked the constant companionship and the attention. All she had to do was think of being hungry or thirsty and Belle, Beau's housekeeper, would show up with treats for her. Maybe it was okay to be pampered until they left for New York.

But that thought made her gloomy. In one week, the girls would be done with their teaching assignment, the lease would be up on the house, and all three of them would be cramming their belongings back into Amy's car for the twelve-hour trip back. And Beau would be staying there, in Myrtle Beach.

"Hi, beautiful."

His normally soothing baritone made her jump.

"That was some deep thought. Did I surprise you?" He slid down onto the couch, his long legs pressed tight to her own. He cupped her breast with one muscular hand while the other teased the back of her neck, his lips against her ear. "I miss you."

Liz knew he was talking about sex but opted to be coquettish. "Miss me? I'm right here, silly." She slid her hand into his lap, cupping his balls.

"Argh." Half moan, half pirate growl, Beau nuzzled her breasts. "They said you have to wait a month."

"I know." She hung her head. "But I'll be in Albany by then."

"Fortunately for me, there is an airport in Albany."

Liz spun to face him as he pulled her into his lap. "What did you say?" She wiggled intentionally, enjoying the pressure his erection gave her bottom.

"Look, I don't want you to go. But I know you have to." She watched his cobalt eyes turn smoky. "And since my schedule is much more flexible than yours, I thought I'd visit. If you'll have me." He traced her lips with his index finger. "You can come down here for the summers and I'll go north once a month until you retire. After that, we can consider other arrangements."

Overcome by the depth of what he'd just said, Lizbeth wrapped her arms around his neck and buried her face to hide her tears. Not only had he been patient and gentle when she'd accused him of cheating, but he'd taken care of her since her episode of amnesia.

Beau gently slid her off his lap and stood from the

couch. With an outstretched hand, he pulled her up and led her out to the back porch.

Surrounded by the hot, salt air, the song of the ocean reached them on the perpetual breeze. His strong arms wrapped her from behind, holding her tight to his chest, his lips nuzzling her ear. "I don't want to lose you ever again. Those four days when you wouldn't speak to me were torture."

She started to protest as he turned her around, trying to apologize for her mistake. But, he shook his head and placed his fingers across her lips and wouldn't let her speak. Then he kissed her. But not one of his teasing, bring-on-the-sex-capade kisses. He lingered, gently nipping her lips, his tongue conversing with every inch of her mouth. A deep, long kiss.

And when he drew back, Liz nearly cried out in shock when he dropped to his right knee, her left hand safely tucked in his. "I love you, Lizbeth. Please say that you love me, and you'll spend the rest of your life with me."

Without hesitation, she leaned forward and cradled his face in her bosom, his kisses warming her soft flesh. "Yes. Yes. And yes!"

She was still laughing when he scooped her into his arms and left the porch. "Now, let's go play in the water."

# Afterword

Dear Readers –

I hope you've enjoyed this beach side romp in my "Passion" series. The next spot we're travelling to is Scotland. We'll be celebrating Hogmanay in the medieval beauty of Edinburgh and then fall prey to the rural charms of Inverness and Oban in *His Highland Passion*.

We're all busy people trying to squeeze as much into each day as possible. Thank you for sharing my love of writing and allowing me to soak up some of your spare time.

Fondly -
    Gracie

## About the Author

Gracie Guy has been blessed with an eclectic and rewarding life, filled with family, friends and a passel of animals. She's a wife, sister, aunt, farmer, runner, skier and gardener, who proudly calls Upstate New York her home.

Find Gracie online:
www.gracieguy.com

## Also by Gracie Guy

A Fragmented Journey

The Journey Creekside

Her Irish Passion

Made in the
USA
Middletown, DE